# Opal

## RARE GEMS SERIES BOOK 4

# KATHI S. BARTON

# WCP

## World Castle Publishing, LLC
Pensacola, Florida

Copyright © Kathi S. Barton 2014
Print ISBN: 9781629891606
eBook ISBN: 9781629891613
First Edition World Castle Publishing, LLC, September 26, 2014
http://www.worldcastlepublishing.com

### Licensing Notes

Cover: Karen Fuller
Editor: Maxine Bringenberg

# Chapter 1

Opal was enjoying Paris. She'd never traveled before outside of the United States, and was having so much fun she decided she might extend her vacation for another month. Who did she have back home to need her? Besides, she'd done really well at the show last month, and she was determined to have a good time before she had to go back and start making things again for the next one. Or, she thought, she'd open her own store. People really seemed to like what she did.

*"Excusez-moi, mademoiselle? Savez-vous où je pourrais trouver l'Hôtel Marcus?"* It took her a few moments to try to translate what the man was asking her. But she beamed when she knew it.

"The Hotel Marcus is on Seventh near the Tea and Crumbles." She hoped that's what she told him anyway when she repeated it in French. When he nodded and stepped around her, she let him go without another thought. People were so nice here.

When she was bumped hard from behind, she turned to say she was sorry. She'd been looking at her map again and sometimes would forget there were others moving around her. But the man said something else to her, and she had a feeling it wasn't nice. When she looked around, she realized that they were alone. Where had all the other people gone?

"You'll come with me, my dear." Opal backed up and blindly put her map in her bag. "Running will do you no good. I've your scent now, and I plan to take you somewhere we can…talk."

"No. I don't know who you are, but I'm not going anywhere with you." She saw a second man coming out of the alley, and he didn't look all that happy to see her either. "I'll scream."

"And who do you suppose would hear you? I've protected you from the tourists around here. It's just you and me. And I do not like to be told no." The man was coming faster now, but he seemed to be so far away. Opal had a thought that the man in front of her had no idea about the one behind him, and decided that she didn't want to go with either of them. Turning on her heel, she took off running until she hit a wall. No, not a wall, but another man.

Looking up into the face of the man that held her to him, she felt a little faint. Men like this one just didn't touch women like her. She tried to struggle away from him, but he snapped at her to be still.

"Sloan? What are you doing here? I thought you were firmly entrenched in the States." They didn't seem to be friends, and the man from the alley confirmed it when he grabbed the first one around the throat with his massive arms.

"I think you know why I'm here. And you'll leave her alone. She's not yours." The man looked confused as Sloan continued. "You touch any of the women from this pack and I'll personally tear your heart out."

"As far as I know, this little morsel isn't claimed. And her virginal blood will make me feel like a man who had dined on the finest of meals and drank of the most delicious liquors. You would deny me that?" Sloan pushed her behind him, and she started to run again. But he grabbed her arm just as the man continued. "I will have her, Sloan. You've no right to keep me from her. A meal is a meal, as you well know."

"You'll leave her alone, as I have said, and she is mine." The man looked shocked, and Opal didn't blame him. She no more belonged to him than she did to either of them. Before she could tell either of them she was her own person, Sloan pulled her in front of him so that she faced her attacker.

The air around them seemed to grow thick. Opal opened her mouth to say something when she felt her hair being let down. Sloan moved his hand through her tumble of curls, and she felt her body light on fire. Nothing had ever made her feel this way before, and his touch was heating her up more.

When a moan spilled from her lips, she put her hand over Sloan's to stop his movement to her breast. But he cupped her hand into his and moved it with his to cup her. Her nipples hardened in her bra, and she moaned again.

"I'm going to taste you." She nodded, not caring what he did so long as he didn't stop what he was doing now. "Come for me, Opal, while I taste you."

Her hair was suddenly moved from her shoulder, and Sloan tilted her head. Opal felt his cock harden against her. And when he rocked into her, she grabbed his arm. Christ, she was going to have a climax if he kept this up. Before she could protest, she felt his tongue touch her pounding pulse, and she tried to tighten her legs together to get some relief there. When she felt the sharp pain of his bite, Opal cried out. Not from pain but from the release that rocked through her entire body.

"*Again,*" he told her in her mind. "Come for me again so that I can taste it." She had no choice in the matter, and her body reacted violently to his command. She was still trembling with sated relief when he licked her again, sealing the wound he'd inflicted.

"There, she's marked. You'll leave her alone from now on." Opal found herself suddenly standing alone and Sloan near the man. It took her fuddled mind a few seconds to realize what he'd done to her.

He'd marked her. Marked her so that the other man wouldn't touch her. Staggering back a little, she heard someone say her name, but she was humiliated enough. She turned this time and took off running. Christ, what had just happened?

Sitting in her hotel room twenty minutes later, Opal tried her best to tell herself that it was all a dream. She'd been hot and thirsty. Not drinking enough could make a person see and think things like that, she told herself. When she finally stood up and went to the bathroom, Opal stripped off all her clothes and stepped into the hot spray of the shower. Washing her entire body three times did not make her feel any less like it was anything but the truth. She'd been bitten and marked.

Getting out of the shower, she dried herself. Opal was nearly through with her first list of things to pack up when she realized that she was leaving Paris today. The appeal of the place was no longer there, and she knew that she had to go home. When she stepped into the living room, she wasn't overly surprised to see Sloan and the man from the alley sitting in her living room. Ignoring them, she picked up her things and took them back to the bedroom. There was no way she was going to acknowledge either of them. When the door clicked shut behind her, she stiffened but didn't stop packing.

~~~

Sloan watched her fold her shirts and pants and put them into the suitcase. He wasn't sure what he was supposed to say to her, because every line of her body told him she was mad and ready to tangle with him. And while she did, he had a feeling she was going to have nothing on her sisters when it came to having a temper. He cleared his throat, trying his best to soothe her, but she seemed to be very focused on what she was doing instead of him.

"I had to do something. He was going to take you. And my biting you saved you from being his whore." She said something, but he was sure he didn't hear it correctly. "What did you just say?"

"I said, so now I'm yours. Your whore." Sloan felt his temper rise, but he calmed himself with the knowledge that she had no idea what he was to her. "I'm thinking I'd very much like for you to go away. I'm going...I've got a great deal to do today, and I want to be alone."

"I have to talk to you." She turned then, and he had only a second to realize he'd been wrong. She wasn't just mad. She was spitting pissed off, and her wolf was coming. But it was her beauty that took his breath away. Before he could say anything, she had him pinned to the wall and several feet off the floor.

"You'll leave me alone or I'll tear your throat out and spit in your face." He wanted to point out that she was very bad at verbal threats, but she was just fine in the scary department. But he had a feeling, verbal or not, she'd kill him if he didn't do something quickly.

*"I'm your mate."* Her body seemed to freeze as he spoke through their link. *"I don't want to be, but you're mine until I can figure out a way to stop it."*

"You marked me." He nodded without much movement. She had him held that tightly. Then she tossed him across the room, and he landed on a chair, shattering it to splitters. He had a moment of worry that all the tales of being unable to harm one's mate were untrue. But she was suddenly across the room, too, when Rufus knocked her away.

Sloan was on the man in a heartbeat, and if Opal hadn't have cried out, he might have killed him. When he turned to her, she had a piece of glass in her chest that she'd gotten when she hit the glass that had been sitting on the table. Christ, there was so much blood...he was at her side immediately.

"Get back." Sloan ignored her and picked her up. She weighed nothing. He wondered if he could convince her to put on some weight before he bit her again. Shutting down that thought because there wasn't going to be any more biting, she cried out again when he tried to look at her wound. Pulling out the glass only made her bleed more, and he knew in that moment that there was no way they were walking away from this unscathed.

"You need to take my blood." The look on her face might have been funny if the situation wasn't so serious. She was losing blood much too fast. He realized she'd cut into an artery. "Opal, you're going to bleed to death if you don't drink from me."

"Fuck off." When she tried to sit up again, he had Rufus hold her. Sloan was actually afraid she'd shift. If she did with the amount of blood she'd lost, it might be her certain death. Tearing into his own wrist, he pressed it to her mouth and commanded her to drink. It wasn't until she was unconscious that he was able to get her to take it. Christ, she was going to die if he didn't do something quickly.

"You're going to convert her if you give her much more." Rufus knew as well as he did that she was dying. "Might save her, but she's going to kill you if you do this."

He had no choice. Sloan either had to convert her to a vampire or she'd die. Neither was an option that he was thrilled with, but letting her die was out of the question. Her family would most assuredly kill him if he did.

"Christ, she's going to hate me for this." He leaned to her throat and bit her hard. Drinking from her as she took his blood was the only way now. When he felt her body begin to take his blood and use it to change her, he sealed the wound at her throat and pulled his wrist from her mouth.

"She's gonna make it, I'm thinking. Might be hard on her with her being so young and all, but I'm thinking you'll pave the way for her. Too bad you lied to her about the mate thing." Sloan stared at his friend until he realized the truth. "Mother fuck, she's your mate? You just fucking converted your mate not an hour after you met her? She is going to kill you."

Sloan ordered Rufus out of the room. His laughter was putting him on edge, and he was terrified enough as it was about this. Looking down at the lovely woman on the bed, he wondered how he was going to tell Blair and the rest when he felt the man touch his mind.

"*You fucking bastard.*" Sloan nodded his agreement at the man. "*I'm going to fucking murder you in your fucking tomb when you get here. I swear to Christ you're going to wish for the sun when I'm finished with you.*"

*"I already do."*

# Chapter 2

Blair stood by the terminal entrance waiting for the couple to disembark. He was still in a murderous mood, but now he had a little more control over it...not much, but a good deal more than he'd had earlier. He looked at Sapphire when she walked up beside him. Her belly was swollen with their first child and he'd never been happier. Murderous, but happy.

"You kill him and she'll never forgive you." He knew that, but it didn't stop him from wanting to do so. "And if you hurt him, she's just going to be in a worse mood than she is right now. I've heard that the two of them have been doing nothing but fighting since she woke up. She's not speaking to him and talking to me since they got on the plane."

"Serves him right. Mother fuck, I could kill him right now in front of all these people." Sapphire nodded but didn't say anything. The plane they were waiting for had landed over twenty minutes ago and yet no one, not even the pilots, had gotten off. He could see the stairs just near the open door. "What the hell is going on? Did she say?"

"Sloan is trying to get Opal to talk to him and he's holding her back from seeing us. I think he's sort of afraid of her." That made Blair smile. "Not to mention, she's still trying to get her feet. The other man, Rufus, he's laughing I guess. And she asked me if she murdered them both if I could help her get rid of the bodies."

"Tell her I'd be glad to help her. Not just with the bodies, but I would gladly take the blame for it." When the stairs started toward the open door, he looked over to see that not only were Thad and Quentin there, but also Jade. None of them looked as if they'd gotten much in the way of sleep. Since they'd been notified of what had happened, they'd all been terrified for her.

The fear he'd felt from someone had been so bad that he'd shifted. It took several minutes of Sapphire screaming at him before he knew that he was scaring her. But when he shifted back, all he could think of was Opal, and he'd reached for her. He couldn't reach her, of course, but Sloan had spoken to him and said he had things under control. What Blair had found pissed him off so badly he was making arrangements to go to Paris before he could think what a bad idea that was.

"He changed her without her permission. I'm really surprised that you're being so calm." Sapphire nodded but didn't say anything. "Are you going to kill him? Is this your way of lulling him into a false sense of security before you tear his throat out?"

"No. What good would that do?" Nothing, he supposed, but it might go down better than this was. "I'm going to talk to him. Then I'll decide if he can live. Otherwise...."

"Here they come." When Quentin spoke, Blair looked at the plane again, and there stood Sloan, but he didn't look all that happy. In his arms it appeared that he had a fighting animal. They had almost reached him before he realized it was Opal.

"Put me down, you moronic ass fuck." Blair had to hide a smile when Opal glared at him. "So, I'm a little weak. I just lost a shit load of blood, and this fucker gave me his. Now look at me. I'm a fucking blood sucker."

"You were dying." Opal looked at Sapphire when she spoke. "You were dying and he had to do something. You of all people should know that as a mate you cannot let any harm come to the other. Behave yourself. You're making people uncomfortable."

Opal didn't say anything, but she did calm. When Sloan sat her down on the floor, he held her until she was steady, then stepped back. It was then that Blair got a good look at her.

Opal had always had a porcelain quality to her skin. Fair skinned, she looked more like a fragile nymph than a full-grown wolf. She was tall, as were all her sisters, but she didn't look it. He supposed it was her calmness, her normal artistic flair that had people thinking she was much smaller than she really was; weaker too. But he knew her to be stronger than most men he knew.

"Have you fed yet?" Opal paled even more at Quentin's question. "I thought not. I don't know a great deal about you and Sloan and your habits, but I'm pretty sure you need to do something. You're beginning to look like you're dead. And I mean that in the kindest way."

"She refuses. And if she continues to be this stupid for much longer, I'll force her again. I don't care for it, but she needs to listen to me. I've had enough of this childish behavior, and I think I've said this to you many times. You will feed—"

"So help me, if you threaten me again, I'm going to tear your tongue out." Sloan looked...well, it was funny how frustrated the man looked. Before Blair could say anything, Opal sat down. "Do you think you can take me home? I'm really tired."

"You'll be coming home with me." Sloan seemed to realize he was shouting, and he took a deep breath and stretched his neck before continuing. "You'll need a safe place to stay from now on. We've no idea what other traits you have, but you will not be able to tolerate the sun like you did before. But knowing you and your knack for being stubborn, I don't doubt you can lay in the sun and it not bother you. Come with me now."

Blair wanted to point out that ordering around a Gem could get your dick cut off, but Opal stood up and he felt his heart break for her. She was weak and getting weaker, and arguing with Sloan was not helping her at all. When Sloan reached for her, Opal nearly fell into his arms as she slid into sleep. He looked at them, so lost that Blair almost felt sorry for him. Almost. The man, as far as he was concerned, was getting just what he deserved.

"I've told her to rest. It's the only way to keep her from harming herself." Blair looked at him hard as Sloan nodded. "She would end her life if I didn't do something. She has...I have had to take precautions that I'm not proud of to keep her safe. Opal isn't...she's not taking this well at all. But I had to save her. She was dying as you know, but she's...she's...."

"She told me she would rather die than to be what you are. And she's not happy about something you said to her in Paris." Sloan flushed but didn't say anything to Jade as she continued. "You hurt her with the other man, and she feels abused by you verbally. What did you say to hurt her this badly?"

"I didn't mean to hurt her. I honestly didn't, but she'd been...he'd taken her, touched her. He was going to take her and she wasn't marked." Jade cocked a brow at him. "Would you rather this mad man had taken her to his lair, fucked her until she was dead, then eaten her for his dinner? It was his plan, you know. And we might have had him had she not acted like a child and taken off running. I had to do something or she'd be victim to some other hapless human. She is most difficult."

Blair laughed, and Sloan growled. "You might want to tone down the order-giving shit if you want this to work out. Also, the name calling? I don't know what she can do as your mate, but whatever it is, she can cause you more harm than anyone else can. She'll be sleeping next to you for a very long time."

"You're no longer upset with me?" Sloan looked hopeful, and the truth of the matter was, knowing that Opal was standing up to Sloan made Blair's anger a whole lot less hot. But did he forgive him? No, not by a long shot.

"I think whatever I feel for you—and none of it is good—is far outmatched by how much Opal hates you right now. I know that's a horrible thing to wish on someone, but I hope she makes you suffer in ways that last a very long time. You terrified us when she was hurt." Sloan held Opal in his arms and nodded at him. "I think for now we should simply get home. There are any number of things that we can say to each other, and they should be said in a place where we can't be overheard."

As they were moving toward their limo, Blair watched a second one pull to a smooth stop just behind theirs. It had no windows over the doors, and the window at the back was so dark that it looked like it was a part of the steel that made the car safe. When a man slipped out of the front and opened the door, both Rufus and Sloan, with his burden, got inside. Blair looked at Quentin when he cleared his throat.

"He has to feed her and figured he'd live longer if no one could see him do it." Blair watched the car pull around theirs and move away. "He said he is going to talk to the counsel at sunset to see about having her removed from being his mate. Sloan thinks that she might be better off without him. I'm not sure either of them will survive much if they keep this up."

"And him? What will happen to him if she isn't his mate?" Quentin didn't say anything but stared after the limo. "Quentin, will he die?"

"I believe that's the plan. He said he's willing to if she will not hate so much." Before he could say anything, if he could even think what to say, Quentin got into the car. Blair thought of what he was saying and felt sorry for the vampire. To have lived so long without a mate; and then after finding one, to have them be the cause of your death. It was heartbreaking.

~~~

Sloan held her in his arms as they made their way to his house. Even in her rest he could feel her weakness and her hatred of him. He looked down at her face and wondered, not for the first time, what the hell he was going to do with her. But Christ, she was beautiful. And as much as he wanted to toss her away, he wanted her in ways he'd never wanted any other woman before…and doubted he would from now on, either.

Her face looked like it had been carved for a china doll rather than a living person; big dark brown eyes, freckles, and a body that invited men—and even some women—to think of silk sheets, sweaty bodies, and nights of screaming out in ecstasy. Sloan tried his best not to think of sex with the woman in his arms, but every time he touched her, every single time he smelled her, he could barely contain his need to strip her down and fuck her. He looked at Rufus when he laughed again.

"You so much as sigh with humor and I will tear your throat out." Rufus nodded and held his mirth, but Sloan wasn't fooled. "She hates me, and you sit there like you are at a comedy show and the headliner is my personal life. You have to know that this is not funny. For either of us. She's going to starve herself to death, and there is little to nothing I can do but force her."

"You gotta admit, she's got herself a hell of a temper. Never seen a little bitty thing like her have so much fury at a single man. And it being you? Well, that just makes it all the funnier. I'm telling you right now, I might just hang out at that house with you two just so I can have me a laugh or two daily. I think she might be getting the better of you more often than not. It's just too funny." He laughed a little before catching himself. "And she can string them curse words together like I ain't never done seen. And her vocabulary? Damn, I'd like to have me a quill and paper to take notes. What was it she called you before we alighted off that there flying contraption? I'm a telling you, that was some name calling there. She's good."

Sloan knew. She'd called him a dicknosed, crotch knob, jockey ass. And he, too, wondered if he should take notes, but he doubted she'd see the humor in it. He was somewhat surprised that she was so full of spit. He'd never met her before the other day, but from what he'd been told, she was the quiet one of the bunch of Gems, and she rarely got mad. She'd been in a constant state of pissed off since he met her.

"What do you know of Fletcher Fleming, or whatever he calls himself now?"

When Opal stirred in his arms, both of them held their breath. She wasn't supposed to be able to wake from his sleep command, but she'd done it before and had been highly pissed when she had. When she settled in his arms again, he held her tighter. His cock stretched in his pants and he had to move her again so she wouldn't wake and find him hard as stone. He knew that wouldn't go over any better this time than it had when she'd woke on the plane with him holding her. Christ, she was a hell fire.

"He's got himself about fifty names. None of them panned out much more'n a few credit cards before about fifty years ago. And since we both have met him, we can rule out him being an old man. One of them was a name that jingled my head but nothing much came out of it. Fleming ain't it though. But it'll come to me." Sloan knew Rufus had a good mind, but he seldom used it. He was more of a crude joke and a mouthy bastard at the same time. "I did find his lair. Not much of one, but the police were right happy with it. I had meself a looksee before they got there and I found a few things you might want to see. Had them sent to your house afore we left. I'm not thinking it's his play one, but it did give me some information that I might get a thing or three from."

"We have to find him. It will go a long way in getting me what I want." Rufus didn't say anything. "What? You don't think I deserve this, do you? I do not want a mate any more than you do. And you're vocal enough about not having a mate that the entire continent knows."

"You got the right of that, sure as shit. But you've done went and made her. Don't that count for much to you? You made me too, but I don't hate you for it. Damn near killed you and you never done much more'n said to behave." Rufus looked at Opal and Sloan felt a murderous rage settle over him before Rufus spoke again. "You done want to kill anybody that touches her. What you think is going to happen when this here thing goes the way you want it to? And short of you dying, I don't really think that's going to change any sooner."

"This is different." He wasn't sure how exactly, but he knew it was. "As for me bonding with her, I had to. You know as well as I do that I had no choice in the matter. It was either give her my blood or let her perish. And the thought of coming back to Blair and the others and telling them that I'd let her die...there was nothing left for me to do."

"Still." Rufus didn't say anything more, but he could almost hear the man thinking. He had changed him, had had to then as well. He'd been his friend before as young men, and when Rufus had been cut open, his belly spilling out onto the ground, he'd simply moved in and changed him. The man had taken a knife for him. It wasn't a choice then any more than the one with Opal had been. It simply had to be done. Rufus had been and always would be his friend. He was crude, sometimes violent, and most of the time not fit for others to be around, but he was his friend and that was enough.

"I'd like you to see what you can find out about the other names you found. Tonight when you rise, we'll go over the things you found and see what we can make out with it. In the meantime, I'm going to see about getting a meeting with the council and see what they can get started." Rufus asked a couple more questions before they stopped in front of Sloan's house. "You should stay here today; well, forever, as I've said to you before. I need you nearby. We work well together, and because I have a mate, it does not change the fact that I like you being around."

"No, I don't think so. When the shit hits the fan, I'm going to be as far away as I can for now. I'm thinking she's going to bring this here house down on your head, and I'd just as soon not be anywhere I can get any of the debris down on me. She's a hell cat; I'll give her that. You should maybe oughta think about taking her. She's fine to look at and with that temper of hers, she'd be keeping you on your toes."

"No thanks."

When he entered the house, he took her directly to his lair. He actually thought about taking her to another room so she'd be able to rest without him in the bed with her, but he was afraid to let her go. After yesterday.... His mind refused to think what might have happened to her had he not woke when he had.

He'd found her standing in the sun when he'd gotten up. It had been full sun coming in the window, but that wasn't what had terrified him. She'd cut both her wrists from palm to elbow. The blood draining from her had been a sight that he'd never forget. She was swaying on her feet, her body already beginning to shut down from starvation. Sloan had never had anything make his heart stutter to a violent stop like that had.

"I don't want to live like this," she'd told him. When he wrapped her into his arms she'd been too weak to fight him. When he held her down with his body, she looked up at him with a wounded look that he knew would haunt him forever. "Please, you can just let me go and no one would know that I didn't die from whatever made you do this to me. Please?"

"I'll know, Opal, and your family would know because I'd have to tell them. I'm so sorry, but I can't let you die." She looked away, and he said her name. "Your family is pissed enough at me. If you kill yourself, they'll blame me."

She stared at him for several seconds before turning away. "Well, we can't let that happen, can we? Let me up. I don't want you to touch me either."

"Opal, I had to save you." She nodded and told him again to let her go. When he rolled off her, she sat up but didn't look at him. "I'm taking you home today. I can't let you continue here with that man looking for you."

"Of course not. I'll pack now." She stood up and turned to him. "I won't try that again, but I'm not going to be your mate. You can do whatever you think to keep me safe until we get to my family's house, but I won't ever be your mate. You took something from me and I'll never get it back. I wanted to be as normal as I could, and you took that all away from me."

He'd let her go, and true to her word, she hadn't tried again in the next twenty-four hours, but that didn't mean he didn't watch her closely. He was sure she was talking to her sisters, but there was little they could do for her from the States. But now they were home, his home, and he was going to talk to someone about having her removed as his mate. It was either that or she might die at her own hand. Sloan stared at her as he stripped down to his naked body.

"I'm not going to take you." He grimaced when he looked down at his straining cock. Even though she couldn't hear him, he was still slightly embarrassed that he was so incredibly hard and wanting her. "I know this looks bad, but I promise you, I have no intentions of taking you. I will have to feed from you, but there will never be anything more than that. And as soon as possible, I'm going to have this thing between us voided; then you can go back to your normal life, and I can go on with mine." He tried his best not to notice how badly that hurt him. He had considered himself very normal, for a vampire anyway. And even though few knew his origins, he was quite pleased with his life until now.

Sloan lay down beside her and laughed when she rolled to the other side of the bed. Even in a deep sleep she knew better than to snuggle up to him. As he tried to get his body and his cock to shut down, he thought of the way she'd tasted to him earlier. Then he sat up on his elbow and pulled her to him.

Tearing into his wrist, he pressed his open vein over her mouth. She tried to turn away again and again, but finally he held her tightly to his body as he commanded her to drink. Her firm ass fit so perfectly against his cock that he moaned when he rocked into her. He had no intentions of taking her, but there was no reason why he couldn't enjoy having a lovely naked woman so close to him.

When she finally drank, her hands wrapping around his arm as she suckled at his wrist, he felt his cock fill to the point of being painful. When he rocked again and again, promising himself that he would stop soon, he nearly came when she moaned. This was not helping him and he wanted some relief, and soon.

"You're killing me." Sloan licked her throat, then nipped gently at her flesh. "Right now all my good intentions are going out the window, and I want to lift you over my cock and fuck you hard."

Her second moan had him pulling his wrist away and sealing the wound. He knew that if he lay there much longer they were going to mate, and neither of them would be happy about it. But when she reached between them and wrapped her fingers around his cock, Sloan stilled. Christ, if she did so much as moan right now, he was going to flip her over and take her like he wanted.

"Fuck me." He moaned at her sleep-filled words. "Just fuck me, honey, and I'll scream out your name."

"Who am I?" Her fingers were dancing up and down his shaft, and he had to hold her still or simply come all over her. "Who am I, Opal? Say my name."

"My vibrator. I'm not sure when you started talking, but fuck me, baby. Make me come like you always do." He felt his cock leak in her hand at the thought of her pushing a vibrator into her own pussy while he watched. "Fuck me so I can relax."

"Christ." He jumped from the bed when she slid her fingers into her pussy. When she turned to stare at him, her eyes wide with something akin to fear, he stood there holding his cock in his hand. He had to have her, yet knew that if he did, they were both going to regret it.

"I want to come. Jerk off while you watch me." His voice tore from him, it seemed, and he fisted his cock when she didn't say anything. "I need to come. Show me what you do when you need relief."

"I don't know what you're talking about. Sometimes I just need a little something. I come quickly, and then I can sleep." But she lay to her back while her fingers worked busily at her pussy. Her breaths were short pants that he could almost feel across his cock. "I'm going to come."

Her scream nearly had him tear his dick off in his haste to join her. Sloan fisted his cock so hard and so fast that he shot his cum all the way across the room and it splashed on her breast. He moved to her to lick it off before he could think not to. Her nipple slid into his mouth and he nipped hard at it to draw just enough blood to feed from her. She cried out again when he joined his fingers with hers.

*Come again. Come with me fucking you like this.* She nodded, and her body bowed up as she screamed out his name. Sloan sat up then and took his cock in his hand and came all over her this time. He watched as it spread all over her hot body and streamed down over her flesh. Christ, he was hurting worse now than he was before. And he knew that no matter what, it was too late now.

"I need to fuck you." He rolled her to her belly and lifted her hips up. Her ass looked like a heart, and he slammed his cock into her heat just as she screamed again. This time he knew it was from pain, from her virginity being taken so violently. He pounded her hard until he felt her body adjust to him. When he came this time, he leaned over her and bit deep into her shoulder. Then she came, tightening her body around his cock. Sloan knew as surely as he was deep inside of her that he'd fucked up royally.

Sloan sealed the wound he'd made but didn't move. His cock was still thick with need and his entire body hurt with the need to take her again and again. He knew that she would take it. She was a vampire too, but he also knew that on some level she was in a great deal of pain from what he'd done.

"Get off me." He started to move when she sobbed. "You made me a promise and the first time we're together, you take me like an animal."

"I'm sorry." He moved them on the bed so that he was still behind her but didn't let her go. His cock was still buried in her, and he held her. "I'm so sorry. But the moment I came on you, I knew it was too late."

"So you decided to rape me." He started to point out that she'd enjoyed it as much as he had, but she pulled away from him and he groaned. She was standing near the bed when he reached for her. Christ, she was gorgeous in all her fury. Well, he was pissed off too.

"I didn't rape you. In fact, if you really think about it, you'll know that you reached for me first." He watched her face turn red. "There you see? You know it wasn't rape. Unless you count you raping me."

His attempt at humor failed, and she put her hands on her hips and glared. All he could think about was begging her to let him dine on her pussy, suckle at her lovely breast, and drink from her again while she screamed out his name.

"Stop looking at me like that." He pulled his eyes from her body to look at her face. "You're never going to do that again."

He moved then, lightning fast, until he had her pressed against the wall and his cock inside of her. "Never is a long time, love."

He fucked her slowly, bringing her to peak three times before he took his own release. When her teeth, her sharp fangs, grazed his own pounding pulse, he thought for sure she would bite, but she only cried out as she came again. She held onto him, digging her nails into his skin until he bit her in the throat. This time when she came, she fainted from it. Sloan held her until he thought he could move. She was asleep when he put her to bed a few minutes later.

# Chapter 3

"I see." She didn't, but listened to the man as he droned on about her credit rating — or the lack of one — and the fact that her having the down payment did not make them want to give her the loan she very much needed. They needed more, like something they could take in the event that she defaulted. Or — and this was really stupid — she should have the money in the bank that they could fall back on if something happened. If she'd had the money in the bank, there would really be no need for her to ask them for a loan. Bankers really sucked. She left the bank and sat in her car, wondering what the hell she could do now.

Opal looked at the list she'd made when she'd gotten up. It had taken her a while to find a sheet of paper, but turning left instead of right had led her into one of the biggest kitchens she'd ever been in and a houseful of people she didn't know. The man standing there had simply smiled at her.

The man who had come forward first, Mr. Alex, had handed her not only a beautiful ink pen when she'd asked for it, but a notebook and a small computer. She looked at the computer again as she sat at the large dining room table she was using as a desk. She wanted it, wanted to use it in the worst sort of way, but she knew it belonged to Sloan, and there was no way she was going to take something from him.

"Mistress?" She looked up at Mr. Alex. "There is a man at the front door who is asking for someone to sign for a box that Master Sloan is expecting. Shall I sign for it or will you?"

"It's not my house." He nodded once and looked like he was going to say more, but nodded again before going out. A few minutes later he came in with a small package and sat it on the dining room table. The box had her name on it.

"I would ask that you not open that." She looked up to see Sloan standing in the doorway, leaning against the jamb. "I have no idea what it is or who in their right mind would be sending you something, but don't open it. Or is that like telling you to open it? You're a mite on the stubborn side."

She wanted to open it. Her fingers actually burned to do it, but she pretended to ignore it in favor of her list. When he chuckled, she ignored him as well…that was, until he sat down next to her at the long table.

"I'm very busy." He looked at her list before she could turn from him. She felt stupid for making the kind of notes she had on the list of things she'd formed on her way back home. The picture of the man being hung by his own guts was something she'd never done before, but she was sure that the banker she'd just talked to didn't deserve to die because she had no money.

"He turned you down?" She didn't answer him but played with the pen as he picked up her notepad. "You've been very busy. I had hoped that you'd stay in bed with me and let me wake you by being buried deep inside of you. Or better yet, my tongue fucking you to several climaxes."

"You aren't going to have sex with me again." He only stared at her until she had to look away. "I don't want you to touch me. I know that I've really enjoyed your advances, but I don't want any more."

"Advances? I made you scream several times with your release." Opal felt her face heat up. "I don't want to think that those were only advances, when I thought they were full out fucking. Would you like me to lay you over this table and show you what I can do with my cock?"

Her body heated with his words and she even thought about laying naked over this table while he took her. She looked into his face and could see that he was serious, and wondered for a moment if she reached for his cock if it would be as thick as she remembered it being.

"I don't want you to touch me." A lie, the biggest one she'd ever told but a lie all the same, and she was pretty sure he knew it. "I would like to be able to conduct my business in private if you don't mind."

"I can give you the money you need." She shook her head. "It's not doing me any good where it's at, and I want to do this for you. I hurt you last night."

"I'm not a whore." He started to speak, but she cut him off. "If you think that paying me for having sex with you makes me anything less, you should look up the word. I'm not going to be your whore any more than I would have been had that other guy taken me."

"You would have been his dinner. When he finished fucking you with more than just his body, he would have flayed you alive and kept you long enough for you to watch him eat whatever part of you he cut from you. And as a half-breed, as you are, he would have enjoyed the rarity of your blood as well as the taste of your meat. Then, when he was satisfied that you understood whatever it was he was doing, he would have slit your throat and rubbed your blood all over his body as he jerked off." She felt her body weaken with the fear of it, but when he reached for her, she smacked his hand way. "I'm sorry. I shouldn't have said those things to you. But when you act like a baby, I want to treat you like one."

"I'm not a child but a grown woman." He eyed her up and down, and she felt her body respond to him in ways that had her squeezing her thighs tighter together. "Leave me alone, please?"

"I can't. You know that as well as I do. We're a mated and bonded couple, and there is little to nothing we can do about rectifying that now." He stood up and towered over her. "I'm going to find out what Rufus sent to me. I'd very much like it if you'd let me feed you again. As for the package, I'll have Alex take it away. It might be harmless, but as no one but your family knows you're here, it might well be something that could harm you." He picked it up and handed it to Alex as soon as he walked into the room. He was gone again before she spoke to Sloan.

"You have to know by now that I don't want to be a vampire. And I'm not willingly going to bite anyone." She watched as he stretched his body out; the long lines of him made her mouth water. When her fangs dropped, he growled low, and she stood up when he told her to. "I don't want this."

"You do and you know it." He tilted his neck, and she watched as he ran his finger over his pounding pulse, leaving a small trail of blood in the wake. "If you bite me like this, maybe I'll be able to not take you to the table and give you the satisfaction that we both crave. Because, as much as you say you don't want to make love with me, you need me as much as I do you."

He took her to his body, wrapping her up in his arms in a way that she could feel his cock at her pussy. When she shifted on her feet, trying hard to pull away from him and his body, he cupped her ass and lifted her to him. She bit him even as he lowered her to the table.

Sloan rode her slowly as his blood filled her mouth and body. There was something erotic tasting about him, and she curled her arms around his neck to hold him there while she drank. They were both still fully dressed, but it mattered little to them, it seemed. She would have easily let him take her at that moment, and there was little she wanted to do about it.

"Christ, I need to be inside of you." Her clothing was torn away, and she felt his cock at her entrance. "I want to drink from you so badly, taste that pretty pussy of yours to see if your juices are as wonderful as your blood. But the need to take you, fill you with my cock, is making me crazy with need. Please, let me take you."

As an answer, Opal wrapped her legs around him as he filled her. Every part of her body seemed to feel him as he became one with her. When he rocked deeper, taking her breath away, she lifted her head from his throat and looked at him. He had blood on his lip, and she pulled it into her mouth and sucked him clean.

"Come." She detonated twice more after he told her to come the first time. Her nerve endings seemed to come alive, and her blood heated to a point where she felt it even in her heart. Her mind, usually so calm and orderly, simply shut down and filled with the release that she had. As she was building up again, he lifted his body from her and stood over her. She nearly cried out when suddenly she was up and leaning over the table, with her ass being slapped by him.

"Don't do that." He laughed when she backed to him. "I mean it. I don't want you to—"

Her climax ripped from her when he pressed his finger into her ass. She roared out when he fucked her with both his hand and his cock. And when she felt his teeth drag across her shoulder then sink into her, Opal screamed again. Sloan came hard, fucking her with quick, hard punches that moved her and the table across the room. Never had anything ever felt this way; nothing would ever have prepared her for such an all-consuming reaction to reaching a peak during sex. When he lay over her, breathing hard and his heart pounding hard, he held her as he sat back in the chair with his cock still deep in her pussy.

"I keep telling you no, yet you take me again and again." He didn't bother saying anything to her, and she felt tears start to fill her eyes. "I don't want you. My body does, but it's not the same."

"I'm aware of that." She started to pull away from him, but he held her. "We have to figure out how to make this work, Opal. I need you as badly as you need me to survive now. I have noticed that you can tolerate the sun, and that's more than likely due to the fact that you're still wolf, too. But I cannot keep you safe if you're constantly starving. I need to protect you. You have to help me or we'll both die. And I don't want anything at all to happen to you."

"I can take care of myself." This time when she tried to stand, he let her. She was under no delusions that he'd let her, either. He was a vampire, an old one if she thought about what he could do in comparison to any of the others that she knew. When she reached for her clothing, in shreds now, he laughed. The thought of ramming the pen into his head made her breath catch.

"In my haste, I destroyed your pretty things. I'm profoundly sorry for that. I'll buy you more things. Just place an order with Alex, and he can make sure it's there when you next rise. If you need something sooner, just tell him so." She didn't answer him, knowing that she'd not be doing any such thing. And she was pretty sure he knew it.

As he left the room, naked as the day he was born, she let the tears finally fall. It wasn't until Sapphire touched her mind that she had any idea why she was crying. She just sobbed harder when her sister asked her if she wanted to go shopping.

~~~

The mall wasn't busy this time of the evening. The usual bunch of high school kids were running around, but nothing like it was on the weekend. But little of that mattered when she looked at Opal. Her sister was hurting. Any fool could tell that, and Sapphire was not a fool.

"Thanks for going with me." Opal nodded but still said nothing. "I have to get me a few more blouses to wear until the baby comes, and I'm sick to death of the ones I have now. Just a few more weeks to go. Then I can pop this thing out and get on with my life while he stays with Blair all day in the hot, stuffy office."

"I think you look great." Her compliment felt halfhearted, but Sapphire didn't say anything as Opal continued. "Wait, did you just...? I was paying attention, Sapphire. I'm just a little distracted, that's all. Can I...? I was wondering if I could borrow some money. I tried the bank, but they said without credit I can't get any. Stupid, I know, but I can't think of any other way of getting this thing going. I'm tired of just doing this half assed."

35

"I'm glad to know you don't think I'd leave the baby like that. And I'd say you're more than a little distracted. As for the loan? You know I can't do that." Opal nodded and moved away from her to another stack of maternity tops…not far, but enough that Sapphire felt the gap. Things were on sale, of course, but the season was all wrong. She watched Opal as she picked up another shirt, this one in a puce color. "Will you tell me why you won't ask Sloan for the money? I know for a fact that he has it."

"I don't want him, much less his money." Her voice was hard and curt, but her actions told Sapphire that she was afraid of something, and she wondered for a moment if Sloan had hurt her. "He and I are mated now. As if you couldn't tell. But I still don't want him in my life. I was doing just fine without him."

"I can tell that you're mated, and congratulations on that. But…how do you feel about that? Because for as much as you say you don't want him, it's obvious that the two of you are making love." She could also tell that her sister had fed, and fed well. She wondered briefly if she'd killed anyone to do it, but remembered what Quentin had told them. They could only feed from each other for the first few months of their bonding, then they could feed from anyone. It was a bonding thing only vampires could understand, he said, something about the safety of mankind. Sapphire thought it was safer; this was just her opinion, but knowing how difficult it was for a mated couple to keep their hands off each other, it was definitely safer for the public that way. Not that her and Blair had started to slow. But lately…well, she was nine months pregnant. Opal turned to look at her before she spoke.

"I hate him. Not to say the sex isn't wonderful, but I don't like him at all. And he feels the same about me. He only did this to save me from being claimed by the other killer." The wording of her last statement had Sapphire still in her next question. Then Opal continued. "He's a blood sucker, and he's made me one."

"As I've said to you before, you were dying. There was no choice; unless, of course, you wish you would have died that day. Missed the birth of your nephew, or even worse, left us all hurting because you were gone. What's really wrong, Opal? You're not pissed because you're alive, are you? Because if you try to tell me that, I'm not going to believe you. Sloan may or may not want you as a mate, but we both know that you've claimed him as well as he has you. Is it the fact that your life has changed so much? Or do you just enjoying being a martyr? Because from where I'm standing, you look like a spoiled child having a temper-tantrum."

Opal turned on her so quickly she couldn't get away, and as she held her above the ground by her neck, Sapphire didn't struggle. After a few seconds, she saw the look in her sister's eyes...realization of what she was doing: horror, and worst of all, fear. Sapphire was let down gently, and then Opal ran from her. It was all Sapphire could do in her huge state to keep up with her. When she caught her, Sapphire pulled her into a chair in the food court. If she was honest with herself, she'd been just a little afraid herself.

"You should get away from me, get as far from me as you possibly can. I'm a monster. And I hurt you. How can you even want to be around me? How can you...what if I hurt the baby? I'm the worst kind of animal, and I hate me." Sapphire was hurting, but not from what Opal had done to her. Before she could tell her that, Opal started crying, a great sobbing cry that had Sapphire reaching for their grandmother. She was at a loss as to what to do. She told her everything.

*I'm coming there now. I had a feeling something was off, and have been milling around this…I have no idea what this store is selling. Sex is all I can think of. What on earth would make a woman go in here and purchase such things?* Sapphire asked her the name, and she laughed when her grandmother told her the name of Sapphire and her sisters' favorite store. *If you tell me you shop here, I shall never speak to you again.*

*All right, then I won't tell you I have a charge card there, and that Blair buys me things there just so he can tear them off me.* Her grandmother sputtered, and Sapphire told her that Opal was hurting, and badly. *I don't know how to help her. And I'm pretty sure she's afraid of Sloan, or at least the life he's given her. What am I going to do to help her?*

*The only thing you can do, love. Love her. But as for Sloan? He won't harm her. I think he's mostly afraid of you in the event that would happen. But he won't harm her.* She could see her grandmother coming toward her, and she had a little pink bag over her arm. Sapphire started laughing. "I had to purchase something after simply standing there for so long. But I swear to you, if you tell anyone that I even went into that place, I'll ground you for a month."

"Grandmother?" Opal stared at her, and Sapphire shrugged when Opal looked at her. "You called her when I hurt you?"

"As I have been trying to tell you, you didn't hurt me. I'm a grown woman about to give birth to this child. I can take on a temper tantrum of a newborn vampire." Sapphire smiled gently at her sister. That's when she saw Sloan coming toward them. "But I'm reasonably sure that your mate thinks I hurt you. Here he comes now. Try not to scream at him when he gets here. I'm pretty sure we'd get thrown from this place, and I happen to love the shops."

He stood over Opal and only stared at her. Sapphire wondered if he realized yet what an imposing figure he made when he did that. But apparently her sister didn't think so and stood up to him. He took a step back, but Opal advanced until he bumped into the table behind him. The man was in love with her, she suddenly realized. Sloan loved her sister and would...Christ, he was hurting as much as Opal was.

"Did I not tell you to leave me alone?" He started to nod, Sapphire thought, but Opal poked him in the chest as she continued. "I'm quite capable of taking care of myself. What do you have, minions running around after me so that you can keep tabs on me? If you do, I want you to call them off. I'm a wolf and have been keeping myself safe for a very long —"

"I don't have minions...not looking after you, anyway. I know better after the last time I sent Rufus after you. But I could feel your terror." That shut her sister up, but Sloan wasn't finished. Sapphire wanted to ask about what happened with Rufus, but Sloan continued before she could. "I could also feel your anger, as well as the murderous feelings you had for a few minutes. Did you kill someone? Not that I don't think we could handle that, but I'd hate for someone to find a body in this lovely mall. But as I see no blood, I can only assume that you —"

"I didn't kill anyone. Not that I'm not thinking about it right now. Would you like to be my first victim? I'm sure I'd feel a great deal better even if I could simply hurt you. A lot." Opal started to turn from him but poked him in the chest again. "What do you mean, you could handle it? Are you saying you'd cover up a murder that I did?"

"Of course I would." Sapphire couldn't see Sloan's face, but she could her sisters, and the look on her face told her that he'd shocked her. "You're my mate. I have no choice but to protect you. And that protection extends to helping you rid yourself of the bodies if need be. I am but your humble servant."

"So you don't really want to protect me, but you would because you had to." He started to speak again, but Opal cut him off. "You know what? This is just stupid. I don't want you here. I'm having a nice time with my sister and grandmother, so you can just go do whatever it is you were doing. I'm just fine and dandy."

Sapphire watched him. Sloan was trying his best not to do something, but she was reasonably sure he was going to lose the battle. When Opal turned this time to walk away, he pulled her back and to his body. They had enough people staring at them right now; if he took her, as it looked like he was going to do, they'd never be able to come here again. But he only held her to him and nothing more for a good long time.

When he spoke this time, Sapphire didn't know what he was saying. It wasn't that he was speaking low that had her not understanding. It was the language. Whatever it was, whatever he said, Opal didn't understand either, she'd bet.

Sloan let Opal go, then walked to Sapphire. He sat at the table for several seconds before Opal joined them. The tension around the table was as thick as anything she'd ever felt. And when Sloan spoke this time, she could hear the barely-controlled anger in his voice.

"She will need clothing. A great deal of it." Sapphire nodded. "I have put her name on my accounts, but she is...she is.... I have to ask you to keep an accounting of what she needs, please, so that I may purchase it for her."

"I don't want—" He cut Opal off with a look, and, surprisingly, she shut up. Sapphire glanced at her grandmother, who was laughing quietly but hard. Tears were streaming down her cheeks as she held her hand over her mouth. There was no help there, of course.

"I can give you a list, but I doubt very much she'd wear it if you bought it for her." He nodded and turned to her grandmother. The smile he gave her was forced, but at least he was trying. But his words were chilling to say the least.

"I have some news for you both. I'm very sorry, but your home was broken into tonight." They both stood up and he asked them to have a seat. "Quentin and the others are trying to salvage what they can, but I'm afraid that the house is in a shambles. Not a loss, but still it has been torn apart. It is fixable, just messy. And most of the things that were destroyed belonged to Opal. So even if she refuses to wear what I purchase, she has no other choice."

"Did anyone get hurt?" He shook his head at her question, but Sapphire knew there was more to it than he was saying at the moment. "Where is Blair? Why hasn't he...did something happen to him?"

"He is fine now." That didn't make her feel any better. "I have been sent to bring you home. I assure you, all is well with him other than I think him to be more related to Opal than you are. I've never ran into a more stubborn family in all my years. He said that you were to finish shopping and to purchase something pretty for yourself. Blair wants to have the house set to rights before you get there."

"I'm going home right now." He nodded and put his hand on her arm. She was standing in their bedroom before she could utter another word. Blair was just coming out of the bathroom, and Sloan had disappeared again.

"I'm just fine." Sapphire ran to his arms anyway. She could smell the fear on him and feel his pain, but nothing much more than that. He held her while she touched him everywhere she could reach.

"Who was it?" He told her he didn't know. "Then why are we up here and not out trying to find the bastard?" His laughter made her realize just how stupid she sounded.

"He left a message for Sloan and his mate." Sapphire sat down. The baby kicked her hard in the belly, and she rubbed her hand over him to sooth him. She wondered if it would be any better had she had him in her arms when Blair continued. "He was the man that found her in Paris, but I didn't catch his name. He'd followed her from New Orleans and had hoped to take her there, but she was being followed and he had to wait. She will be watched more closely now, he said, and I would take that as gospel. Sloan was terrified when I called him."

"The body guard that Sloan put on her, Rufus? Is he the one that is keeping her safe? And Sloan, too, I would guess?" Blair nodded. "Tell me what it said, this note; tell me what he said about my sister."

Instead of answering her, he handed her a thick envelope. She almost wanted to tell him she'd changed her mind, but took it. As soon as the first picture spilled out, she looked up at him. When he reached for the rest, she told him she had to see.

They were pictures of Opal. Sapphire was sure if she fanned them just right she'd be able to see the way her sister had been hurt like a movie. And when she saw the blood pouring from her chest and spilling out onto the floor beneath her, she put her trembling hand over her mouth. Sloan really had saved her sister's life. Then the pictures were of another woman, another place, and this time they were only snapshots of the way she was killed, the way her face looked in pain and eventually her death. She put them into the envelope and pulled out the handwritten letter.

*She will die this way. I had her first, my dear Sloan, and when I get her, I will fuck her over and over before I begin to cut her up and have her for my meals. I know you think you have gotten the better of me by hiding her away, but I will find her. And you. I have both your scents now, and you will both suffer at my hands. This you can count on.*

Sapphire looked at Blair. "Does he know this man?" Blair nodded. "Do you think he'll be able to get her? Get her through Sloan? And do you think this...this thing has a snowball's chance in hell of getting past us?"

Blair laughed. "Right now, I'd be more afraid of you than of some faceless stranger. But he has it under control, he said. Sloan said that he'd explain tonight, after the sun was down just a little more. The guy looked like...he was as angry as I've ever seen him. He had to...I'm assuming he had to go and see to Opal. He also told me that it's too late for them to get their union dissolved." She nodded, slightly embarrassed. "So it's true? He had mated and bonded with her. Did he hurt her, you think?"

"No, I don't think so. In fact, I would say that he didn't do anything that she didn't want. Or both of them wanted. She hates him, but I think she hates herself more. I didn't get a lot from her, but I have a feeling she's not taking this as well as I'd think she should." She glanced at the pictures. "I think if she saw those, she'd have a better understanding of how far he went to save her. I wonder how he got them, this person. I wonder how he managed to take these pictures and not help them when she was hurt."

"I don't know. Sloan said he had an idea, but he never shared it. And he said she was never to see them. In fact, I was supposed to burn them after I saw them." Sapphire knew he'd kept them for her to see, and she'd do the same for Opal. She had to know what had really happened in Paris and how much trouble she'd been in.

"And this destruction from today...this is the same man? Do you think that he came here to get her and was pissed that she wasn't here? By the way, what happened to you?" He lifted his shirt up and she saw the long mark on his chest. It looked like something out of a nightmare and she went to him. "Who did this? That man?"

"Yeah, I think he lashed out before thinking about it. Lucky for me, I wasn't alone when we came upon him. Justine was here getting something for the client that Opal had helped me with. We sort of heard him trashing Opal's room. Don't ask me how he got in because I have no idea. But there he was coming out of her room when I went to find a drawing Opal had done for me with the logo you and she were working on. He looked...well, he looked like he thought it funny that I'd caught him. Almost like...I told Sloan this, but he looked like he was relieved that I caught him." Blair shivered and stood up. "He said he was glad to see me again. I had no idea what he was talking about until he lashed out at me. I fell back and the next thing I knew, Sloan was there fighting him. I think he might be hurt, too, but he was suddenly gone and I was picking my ass up off the floor. Do you suppose this guy, this other vampire, is the one that Rufus was talking about a few weeks ago?"

She didn't know, but she was going to find out. The first thing she did was contact her other sisters. Then she called in the other troops. It was war time and she had a family to protect. The moment this bastard had touched what was hers, he was as good as vampire tar-tar.

# Chapter 4

Fletcher woke with a start. He knew that he wasn't in his lair, but where he was—at the moment anyway—eluded him. Then he remembered with full clarity and smiled. Sitting up, he looked around the blood-soaked room. He'd been very busy and he felt wonderful for it.

"You should really clean up after each meal. This room reeks of death." He grinned bigger when he saw his friend and sometimes lover come out of the shadows. "You've been playing at God again?"

"No. I've been playing at being Him. Create, then murder. Isn't that the way we're supposed to do this shit?" He stretched his naked body and wrapped his hand around his semi-hard cock. "Come over here and let me fuck you."

"I'm not in the mood for you to get your jollies off while I get nothing. But I brought you a treat." Fletcher pouted but didn't stop what he was doing. He knew Marvin and also knew that mood or not, he'd suck his dick if he wanted him to. When the man finally dropped before him and took him deep into his mouth, a second person, one he didn't know, stepped up to him. *Drink from her so that I can get my own relief. It's been too long. And I suddenly need me some Fletcher cock.*

The woman was naked, and gloriously plump. Before she could do much more than run her tongue over his nipple, he pulled her to his mouth and bit deeply into her throat. Her blood was spiked with something sweet and he drank greedily. Then it hit him. Faerie.

"She has a friend." Fletcher looked over just as Marvin fell back on the floor, his naked cock straining hard and thick. "I thought maybe if we got this out of our system now, you'd be easier to talk to. I need to have a conversation with you as soon as you are ready. But for now? I think a good fucking is in order. You take as much as you want. I have it on good authority that they're well fed too."

Fletcher nodded and watched as the first woman sat on Marvin's cock and started to ride him. Before he could position himself in front of her, the second woman was in front of her getting her pussy eaten. Fletcher loved pussy, and when two women were getting together, he could rarely contain himself. He watched until he felt left out. Then a pretty blonde came out of the shadows and bent over in front of him; her ass drew him to her like a bug to a light.

Slamming his cock deep into her tight hole, she cried out and came twice before he touched more than her ass. Fletcher liked a thick bottom, and even more so a tight hole to fuck. When she reached between her thighs and played with her clit, he bit deeply into her shoulder and emptied himself into her as she came. Christ, and this was only the beginning. He rolled her over again and had her suck him until he was hard before having her spread wide for him while he fucked her pussy this time.

They continued to switch around between the women and each other for at least another hour. He was relaxed for the most part, but he was well fed when they finally had had enough. When he laid down, both spent and exhausted, he looked over at the mess they'd made of his already trashed room. Marvin laughed when he groaned. There were more bodies to clean up as well as something he didn't want to think about laying just under the corner of his bed. He was sure it was a foot. They'd had a great time, however.

"You need to seriously find someone you can trust to come in here and clean up after you. And maybe you could learn to not kill everyone you fuck." The faeries had been killed, of course, but neither man had any qualms about it. "Do you suppose that will cost us again?"

They'd been warned twice already not to kill a willing faerie. Not that Fletcher gave a shit about the fines they would put on his head, but he hated the bother. The woman who had told them both to behave or they'd have to pay the consequences had told them that they'd suffer like they never had before. Fletcher was pissed because now he'd have to go without their sweet-tasting blood for a decade or two before he could partake again. Then he remembered that Marvin had said he needed to talk to him.

"What did you want? And by the way, I do have a cleaning crew come in when I have a mess. It's expensive and they have to be paid in cash, but they take it all away and leave me with a mint on my pillow." Marvin nodded and closed his eyes, and Fletcher decided to remind him again. "When you got here, you said you had to talk to me. What was it?"

"Oh. Do you know a Sloan Crane?"

Fletcher nodded without looking at Marvin, and the man continued. If he had opened his eyes, Fletcher knew

Marvin would have seen the look of fear on his face, as well as hatred. Fletcher simply hated the man.

"He's got everyone out looking for you. Seems you pissed him off something furious. He's telling people you're up to your old tricks again. I never knew that you stopped, but there you have it. What did you do to shit in his oatmeal?"

"With Sloan there's really not much that won't piss him off. And he's only pissed off because I went to his mate's house and fucked it up a bit. When she got away...well, you know how I am. I hate when I have to leave my dinner walking around. When I went to get me a new toy, Crane and that asshole Rufus was there." Fletcher thought of the big wolf he'd seen there as well, and had to repress a slight tremor of fear. The man had been big, but not only that, he'd gotten too close to him before he'd known he was there. That more than anything terrified Fletcher. It had only happened once before, and Fletcher had a fear that it was the same boy-turned-man who had scared him so badly before.

"You fucked with the alpha too, I guess. There are not just a bunch of vamps looking for you, but a huge fucking pack of wolves. And that guy, the alpha, is no one I'd want to fuck with. Christ, what do you do? Draw names out of a hat and see who you can fuck with daily?"

Fletcher got up and reached for his pants as he thought about what Marvin was saying. He thought about showering but knew there was at least one body in the stall, and he thought maybe there was on the floor as well. Instead of going to check, he simple decided to take a shower elsewhere. He looked at Marvin when he spoke again. Surely this alpha had no reason to come for him. It was just a house, not his fucking family.

"What do you mean, he's gunning for me as well? What possible reason could he give to have me in his sights? Because I tore up a few clothes? Maybe cut him up a little when I was leaving? That is no reason for him to be looking to harm me. If he even could. An alpha has in no way the ability to harm me. None of us." Marvin shrugged. "Who is this guy and what does he think he can to do me?"

"Blair Henson."

Fletcher's skin tightened around his body. It was the same man, the same man who had put the fear of.... And worse yet, this man knew what he was, too. This wolf he'd hurt was not just an alpha and a rich man, but he had powers that went well beyond anything that he'd heard before.

"You know him, I see."

"He's nothing." But he knew that he was. "I had a go around with his father once. Allen Henson. The man was driving me crazy, and I might have gotten a little insane over it. His son, a teenager then, had come at me with everything he had. I nearly...well, hell, I nearly didn't come out on top. And you know as well as I do that I am always the one that is on top. The view is better. But he doesn't know me as Fleming. Back then I was called...."

He couldn't remember. And worse yet, he was pretty sure that Marvin knew just how badly the man had affected him. When he nodded, as if he understood, Fletcher had an overwhelming urge to kill the man who had been his friend longer than most people had lived. But he let it slide from him, roll off his back so that at least someone had his back if things went south. Marvin might be a dork and a dandy, but he could fight like no other vampire he knew.

"I just came here to give you the information and to see if you were a willing fuck. I should have known you'd be willing. You're the only vamp I know that can fuck more than me. And feed too. Christ, we need to do this more often. Next time you bring the food, though. The faeries were just a bonus that I happened to run across." Marvin started to turn away. "There is another guy, Rufus. I think he's a friend of that Crane guy. You know him?" Smiling this time, he nodded. "Thought so. But you should be aware that he's with the group looking for you, but.... Well, he's snooping around too, but seems to have a better angle on things than the rest of them do. You might want to be a little more...." He looked around the room and so did Fletcher.

There were at least two dozen dead or dying bodies around the room. Two were in the big bed they had just fucked the women on, one was in a chair that he had no idea where it had come from, and there were at least two more hanging out from under his bed. The foot he'd seen earlier was, thankfully, attached to a body, but he was still clueless as to how it had gotten there, or even who it might have belonged to. Not that he ever made an effort to know names. They were just food, cock, or pussy to him. He'd had a good time last night, as had these people before he'd killed them. As far as he was concerned, there was no other way to feed than this.

"Are you telling me to lay low?" Marvin shrugged, and Fletcher had that urge again to tear his throat out. He wondered about that for several seconds while he calmed his beast, which seemed to be just on the surface lately. He was glad when Marvin said he was going. Fletcher made his hands unclench and his body relax just a little while he talked calmly to the monster that resided in everyone. "I'll see what I can do. In the meantime, thanks for the fuck. I needed it."

After he was gone, Fletcher made a couple of calls. First and foremost, he called the removal people. He hated messes, and this one was entirely too big for him to ignore while he moved about his household. Fletcher moved to the upper levels of his house and waited to let the crew in while he thought about what his friend had told him.

He'd used this crew for the past six months and so far, they were better than anything he'd ever used before. And by what he'd used before, he meant a dumpster. Fletcher would take the bodies as far from his home as he could go, dump them either in a deep body of water or a trash receptacle, and go about his business. The stains of blood would eventually fade, of course, but he'd been killing more and more lately and it was too much work to do it alone. He didn't have long to wait, as within the hour, they were knocking at his door and dressed like they were going into a hazard-filled building. He supposed in a way they were.

As the crew was removing the bodies, he moved out into the night to see what he could find out. Having Sloan look for him was one thing, but a Henson was too much entirely. The men, the two of them together, were something of an enigma, and not one he wanted to tangle with. He thought about the night he'd first met the younger Henson.

Allen had been alpha back then. Fletcher had been trailing a wolf that he was going to kill when the man, a large man if he remembered correctly, had suddenly stepped from behind the tree and right into his path. Fletcher had actually thought about simply killing the man, but something made him hesitate. Much like his son, the then alpha hadn't had a scent to warn Fletcher of his coming. And that was scary in itself. But this man, Allen, had been a bastard then, and Fletcher had no doubt that his son was more so. He thought to lord himself over Fletcher, and that was what had pissed him off more.

"You will stay off my pack land, vampire, or I will not be responsible for what happens to you when you rest. I know where you lay." Tyson...Tyson Hudson he'd been calling himself then, he suddenly remembered, and laughed. But back then the five big wolves that had also stepped out of the trees had made him take a step back. Fear had not been an emotion that he'd been all that familiar with since changing to a vamp, and it had taken him several seconds to recognize what he was feeling. The younger wolf, related, he knew immediately, to the alpha and bigger than his father, had moved to sit next to his dad. He knew instantly that this boy would be one to be reckoned with.

"So you're going to sic your baby on me? Good luck with that one. Do you have any idea how old I am?" The son raised his nose to the air and then turned to look at his dad. When Allen laughed, Fletcher felt his skin crawl. The finger of fear that he'd felt before widened and slid over his body like a blanket. Cold and wet, he shivered even now from the feelings he'd felt. Fletcher tried to mask it with bravado and anger, but he was pretty sure that none of the pack had believed him. The calmness pouring from the wolves had made him want to run.

"He says you're only a baby. Only just turned one hundred on July twenty-fifth. Congratulations on that one. But I doubt you're going to make it to two if you keep fucking around on my land." He'd said it with such conviction that Fletcher still felt his body strangle around him in fear. But he looked at the big wolf that stood so still in front of him and knew to show him how he was feeling would be signing his own death certificate. He knew for as long as he lived—and he hoped it would be longer than that day—that the memory of that day would remain in his mind as a fear like no other.

The alpha's son was huge, as he saw when the wolf stood up. Even from the standpoint that he was a shifter, he was at least a hundred pounds of pure muscle more than the others there, even the ones older than him in years. His coat was a dark hue, and Fletcher remembered thinking that if he were in the moonlight, it would more than likely glow. But it wasn't just his size and canines that frightened him the most, though those were enough. It was his ability.

No one he'd ever met had been able to tell how old he was. Few people, including himself, could tell what century vampires were born in. It was something that each of them held close to them, because the younger a vampire was, the less they had to combat you with if it came to that. But this young pup had hit it dead on, including the month he'd been born. Fletcher had started forward but was stopped by the low growl coming from the boy. He thought if he could have killed him then, ended the nightmare that started that night, he'd be a much better vampire. But it wasn't to be. And that had come back to bite him fully on the ass.

"You think to let him take me on, old man? This is public property so far as I can see, and you and your little band of dogs aren't going to stop me from coming for you." The air tightened around them and he felt as if he'd been swallowed whole by a fire breathing dragon. When he felt himself being pitched back, he knew sure as shit he was a dead man. After that, he remembered nothing that had happened for five days. When he woke—and he felt like he'd been staked out in the sun—Fletcher had vowed never to set foot on that property again. And now...nearly fifteen years later…Christ, now the man was back for him. And he was no closer to figuring out what had happened than he had back then.

"Mister Fleming? We're finished." Fletcher nodded and handed the cleaner an envelope. He had no idea what they did with the bodies they took from here weekly, sometimes nightly, and didn't care so long as he didn't have to deal with it. When Fletcher walked into his lair, he could see that someone had even made his bed. He was standing under the hot spray of his shower when something else occurred to him.

Blair Henson would know where he was.

~~~

Opal wanted the building, more than she thought she'd want anything in the future, but there was no way she could afford it. When the realtor asked her if she wanted to see the upstairs apartment, she almost told him no, that she'd had enough suffering for one day, but nodded instead. What the hell, maybe someday, right? *Sure*, she thought, *and I'll learn to fly*.

She was nearly to the top of the stairs behind the man when she had a sudden thought. *Could* she fly? Probably not. She had been studying up on being a vampire, and so far most of the things she'd read about were things she could also do as a wolf. They couldn't fly either.

Just that morning she'd tested to see if her wolf was still there, and when she had taken her, she ran for nearly two hours in the woods behind Sloan's house just to be free. It had made her feel normal again, like the person she'd been before. A person who didn't have to drink blood to live.

"There are four rooms up here. The last owner used it as his office work site. I do believe that he has left behind a great deal of the equipment as well as some boards. We were going to toss them out when we cleaned up, but my secretary thought someone who bought the building may have use for them." He cleared his throat before continuing. "Your sister said that you make a line of jewelry?"

"Yes. I have a large selection of fine work." She never really knew what to say to people about what she did, so she quoted the business line that her sister had put on her cards not long ago. Opal knew that she could go on for hours about a piece if someone asked her, but to tell them about what she did was hard for her. "Did my sister explain to you that I was only looking right now?"

He nodded and frowned. She could almost see his mind working. No sale, no sale. She really didn't know why Sapphire had set this up, but it was really nice to dream, she supposed. But after the mall...well, Sapphire might have thought a stroll for what she could have would help.

The equipment left behind was several large drawing boards, a huge desk that she would love to have her grandmother refinish, and several long hardwood tables that she could have used now. But Opal only ran her fingers over the marred surfaces and wished she had the money. Maybe in a few years, she told herself, and wandered around the room for another ten minutes before she looked for the realtor. He was in the main part of the lower floor on his cell phone. When he closed it, she smiled at him.

"I have two other buildings to look at after this. Not with your company but others." She was babbling, and he nodded and frowned again. "Is there something wrong? I mean, if you're upset about showing the building to someone who can't afford it, I can understand, but I think it's more than that, right?"

"No. Yes. It's just that…as the owner of this building, I just assumed that I was helping you with some renovations. I thought you needed me to make some recommendations as to what you needed. I think you have a good head on your shoulders and more than likely know better than I what you want. It was…I'm not sure why I was asked to come here and show you around, but as of early this morning, I was told that the building was in your name. However, I must confess, I didn't know you as Opal Crane."

*The bastard*, she thought. Sloan had done this. She nodded once and told the realtor that she'd be out shortly and asked him if he'd give her a moment. He nodded again, then turned to her and handed her the key. He told her that it was hers and if she didn't mind, he wanted to go back to work. She let him. What good would it do to take her anger out on him?

She thought about calling Sloan. Telling him off would have given her so much pleasure, but not really much in the way of satisfaction. She wandered around the entire building again before she left. Sitting in her car, she wondered what the hell she was supposed to do now. Opal Crane indeed. She wanted to use a crane and drop him from it as soon as she saw him again. But as much as she knew that she wanted to hurt him, she also knew that she couldn't.

Starting her car, she made her way to her sister's house. Everyone she knew would be out of the house and doing either their job or something that took them from the house. Opal drove directly to her little shop. Parking around back, she pulled out her keys and went inside. The sight and smell of it always made her feel just a little better.

She had over three hundred orders to fill from the show in New Orleans. After making sure that her area was neat and orderly again, she had to place orders for more of the supplies that she'd sold out of, and some jewels and chain to finish others that she'd already started. Her boxes also needed to be unpacked and the contents put in their proper places. It was already becoming more and more difficult to have enough room to work and sort her things. When the orders she'd just placed started to come in, she was going to be hurting.

It was nearly one when she started on some of the orders. She was just finishing up the first stack she'd pulled out when the door opened behind her. Opal figured it was one of her sisters and told them to hang on. But when her chair was jerked around, she shifted so quickly that her breath caught between her human and the wolf. The man standing there with his back pressed firmly against the door looked as startled as she was. *Sloan should know better than to startle a shifter.* She could have killed him.

"I've been trying to reach you all day." She growled low at Sloan. "You've been blocking me, and I was…Christ, you scared the shit out of me. Is that the way you normally meet someone? Like the mail guy? Do you shift like that when he knocks on the door to give you a letter?"

*What do you want?* He nodded and pointed to the chair, and she nodded once. Her wolf was still pissy, and she wanted blood. But he sat down, put his hands on his knees, and stared at her. He was looking like he was as calm as they came, but she could feel his fear and wondered about it. *I asked you a question.*

"So you did. I'm simply waiting on my heart to beat at a normal pace and my entire body to…. Did you not like the building?"

Opal sat down and tried her best to ignore him. There was something extremely appealing about him right now, and she couldn't put her finger on it. Watching him carefully, she ignored his question as he had hers. But his laughter startled a low growl from her again, and she glared at him. "I was just thinking about something. And seeing that you didn't strip down, I had a sudden thought. Are you naked? I mean, when you shift...I see your clothing and I can only assume that you're naked. I don't suppose I could persuade you to shift back to a woman and show me. I'd very much like to see you now."

His voice was like a purr, a soft stroke across her skin. She yawned hugely and laid down. Of course, he knew that she was naked. Like he said, her clothing was in shreds all over the floor. But when he stood up and began taking off his belt, she stood as well.

"I can't shift. I can do a great many things, but shifting isn't one of them." The belt hit the floor, and he opened the fly of his pants, then pulled his shirt over his head and dropped it on the belt. "Are you going to shift back for me, Opal? Are you going to go from that amazing wolf to human and let me lay you over this desk and eat you? I haven't yet, you know, and the thought of tasting you has me as hard as stone."

*I want you to leave here.* He sat down and pulled his boots off one at a time and stacked them neatly by his clothes. Then he stood again. *I'm not in the mood for your crap today, Sloan. I have a ton of orders to do and you're in my zone.*

"I'd rather be inside of you. Of course, we could go back to our house. I think taking you on the bed would be fun, but not nearly so much as eating you right here would be." He stood before her, naked, now having taken off not just his pants but his boxers as well. She felt her body respond to him, and when he fisted his cock and moved slowly up and down it, Opal also knew that he could smell her. And as much as she disliked this man, he did give her incredible orgasms. But her wolf wanted him more than she wanted him the hell out of her life.

She moved along his legs, and when Sloan moaned, her wolf growled low...not one of warning this time, but of pleasure. When he sat down again, his cock right at her level, she thought about licking him and decided that was just too weird. Instead, she licked his thigh and nearly cried out when he moved her face to his cock.

"Just a lick. I want to feel you. Wrap that tongue around me and let me feel you. Taste me, Opal, please, I beg of you to taste me." She lapped at his cock and wanted more. His body tasted of heaven. Her wolf moved to his thigh again, but instead of licking him, she sank her canines deep into his thigh and tasted his rich blood. Sloan sat very still after putting his large palm over her head just behind her ears.

Opal expected him to knock her away, and try as she might, her wolf would not let him go. The harder she bit down the more he rubbed his hands through her fur. When she jerked her head, knowing that she was scarring him, he only growled a little but let her mark him.

As soon as she'd had enough, her wolf let him and her go. Opal looked up at Sloan and into his pain-filled face, then at the wound she'd given him. She ran her fingers over the forming scar before looking at his face again.

"I didn't know she was going to do that." He nodded but said nothing. "Are you pissed at her? At me? I really did try to make her stop."

"I know you did. And no, I'm not upset with either of you. She was marking me the same as I did you." Opal nodded but didn't move. "I want you. Now more than ever, I want you. Will you let me drink from you?"

"Yes." He lifted her up so that she was standing with him. Opal looked into his eyes to see if he truly wasn't mad. She was nearly as tall as him, but she always felt so tiny when he was near her like this. His cock, full and hard, slid between her legs and she could feel him at her core.

"Do you have any idea how terrified I was that I couldn't reach you?" She shook her head and started to ask him why, but he continued first. "The thought that someone could have taken you, hurt you, made me insane. I never even thought to look here for you. But I was going to the woods behind this house when I saw your car. All sorts of things ran through my head, and when I saw you sitting there working, I never thought that you'd shift. Christ, you're beautiful as a wolf, more so as a woman."

"You'd be rid of me then. If someone were to kill me. Wouldn't you like that?" He paused and stared down at her for several seconds. "You don't want me any more than I do you, right? I mean, wouldn't that just simplify things for you if I were gone?"

"I don't want you to die." She turned away from his words, but he pulled her back. "I don't want you to die, Opal. I'm not even sure that I want to be apart from you for more than an hour. I need you."

"I know. You need me or you'll die." She moved away from him, and this time he let her. She sat up on her desk after moving back some of the smaller pieces. "But we both seem to enjoy the sex, and I like how you make me feel when I orgasm."

Opal had never thought of herself as sexy, wasn't even sure how to look that way. But she knew that he wanted her, and sat back on the big table and spread her legs. As much as it embarrassed her, Sloan seemed to enjoy the view. She just hoped that no one came into the building right now.

"I have to talk to you about what you just said. I really don't want you to die. And it has little to nothing to do with having to feed from you." She nodded and ran her fingers over her breast and felt her nipple tighten. She didn't believe him. "Do it again. Pinch your nipple until it's hard for me."

"I have a vibrator. I use it sometimes when I can't sleep. It's sort of satisfying. Not like when you make me come, but I do enjoy it." He stepped closer to her and then pulled her chair to sit it between her legs. "I've never...I don't know what to do when we do this. I know that you want me, but I've no idea what to do with myself when you do this to me."

"What do you mean, when I do this? You mean when I eat you?" She nodded. "You're such a wild animal when we have sex, yet you can't say to me — the man who has come deep inside of you — what you want when we have sex. I want to hear it. Please? You're going to have to learn to tell me what you want. Say it for me, Opal. Tell me that you want me to eat your pussy until you come."

She wanted to but felt her face heat. When she tried to close her legs, suddenly too embarrassed to be sitting so exposed, he stilled her legs with his hands. Spreading them wider, he licked his lips and stared at her. As he moved his hands down her inner thighs to her ass, he spoke softly to her.

"You have the most exquisite scent. Not like other scents that I smell on you, but here, right here where I enter you, you smell like the finest wine and the tastiest blood. It's what calls to me when you're needing me. I love the way you wrap around my cock and ripple around me when you come." She moaned when he slid his fingers into her. "You're so wet, baby. Wet and soaking my fingers as I move in and out of you. I'm going to drink very deeply of you."

"Will you bite me?" He stared at her for several seconds, then nodded. If he had set fire to her body, she couldn't have gotten any hotter. The thought of him sinking his teeth into her, drinking not only her juices but her blood, made her nether lips swell around his working fingers until she thought she'd die from the feelings. "Will you drink my blood too?"

"Yes." He leaned forward and slowly licked her. Opal nearly came up off the table, but he settled her with his fingers again. When he opened her wider, sliding his hand under her ass and over her thighs, she knew that he was not going to let her go until he had his fill. This time when he lifted his head, she saw something that she'd never seen on him before. It was both frightening and somewhat arousing.

"My beast wants you as well." She nodded. The red of his eyes wasn't frightening to her. On the contrary, her need for this part of him spiked. "Can anyone hear us?"

"No." He smiled then and she watched, mesmerized as he seemed to expand and shift. His fangs became longer, sharper, his eyes darker as they filled with blood. She heard his heart then; the hard yet steady pounding of it echoed her own. Her body seemed to cry out for his as he leaned down to her. Then he opened his mouth wide and bit.

# Chapter 5

Rufus watched the house. He knew better than to engage on his own, but damn it all to hell and back, where the hell was his back-up? When he looked around again, he saw Sloan coming toward him, and the man looked like he'd just conquered the world...as well as smelling like his mate. Rufus was happy for the man. He wore being happy a hell of a lot better than Rufus ever would.

"Been busy?" Sloan only nodded and leaned against the wall where Rufus had been hiding out for the past three hours. "I've been calling for you for some time. Did you have other things that were more important than getting this feller? You do 'member what he done did to your mate and all, right?"

"I do, as a matter of fact. But this was just as important. I needed to...Opal came up missing and I had to find her. And one thing led to another and...." Rufus could just bet a few things led to more things but said nothing. "She still doesn't like me much. I don't know what to do about that. But I'm beginning to see the appeal of having a mate. Especially one as lovely as her. But still, she does hate me, and I'm at a loss as to figuring out what to do about that."

Fucking her came to mind, but Rufus could see by the satisfied look on his friend's face that he'd done that. A lot. Rufus looked back at the building that this here man was in. He tried to think what he could say to Sloan to get the sappy look off his face, but decided that he kinda liked it there. The man hadn't looked this good in years. He hated seeing him tied up with a damned mate, but it coulda been worse, he supposed.

"I remembered." He glanced over at Sloan as he frowned, but he didn't say nothing. "The jingle to my head. I remembered where the name had come from before. The one I told you about."

"What was the name? I'm assuming that whoever he was, this is where Fleming is holding up now." Rufus nodded, and Sloan started looking at their surroundings and then back at him. "Does he really live here?"

The place looked like a war zone when you first took a looksee, Rufus thought. Then the longer you saw it, the more it began to take on some shape. The house wasn't nearly as bad as it looked, first of all. It was about the only one that looked like a good wind wouldn't take it out, at least on that side of the street. The yard had been mowed, but no flowers or those pretty things that women liked were there. Even the car, the one that rarely got moved, was in good shape. It was very manly in a very quiet way. If you just looked, Rufus knew, you'd think that the entire street was up for repairs, but it really wasn't. It was done to keep others out. He wondered briefly if the place was as fancy on the inside as Sloan's house was.

"Yeah, he does have himself quite a place, huh?" Rufus laughed then. "I ain't never seen a more pompous ass in all my years. Unless'n you count you. When I first met you, I thought you was a fop. Is that what they called dandies back then? Anyway, you was all dressed in that lace and silk. Wondered for a minute or two if you weren't one of them funny guys."

"I have no idea what you're talking about. Funny guys? And I was never a dandy. It was the early fourteenth century. I was in style." Rufus snorted but said nothing as Sloan continued. "Anyway. This house of his...do you suppose he might have a bolt hole to go out if we were to go in the front door? I mean, for all we know, he could be living in all of them and have his room in each of them."

"Nah...he did live in that one there on the corner from what I can tell. It's all boarded up now. I think it was condemned. He might could have a bolt hole, but I gots you a few guys wondering around the back on occasion. Just some bums I talked into helping out." He laughed when Sloan winced. He loved making the man do that, and tried his best to speak as lowly as he could when they were together. "I did find me something you might be interested in. There's been a van here right near every week for the past month, just going in and coming out with bags, like them there body bags. And they'd be full. This morning, they took out a nice round eleven."

Sloan opened his mouth but said nothing. He shook his head, and Rufus laughed. The man was in entirely too good a mood today. Rufus wanted to be jealous, but the alterative was finding a mate, and there was no fucking way he was going down that gravy train.

"Do we know where the bodies—if that's what they are—are being taken after they leave here?" Rufus told him where he'd followed the van to. "So he has a mortuary helping him out. And the clean-up service, do you know who owns that?"

This part he knew that Sloan was going to hate. He'd tried since he'd figured it out to decide how to tell the man, but there was no help for it. Rufus reached into his pocket and pulled out the small scrap of paper and handed it to him. Then he waited for the fireworks. When they happened, Rufus smiled. Better them than him was his way of thinking.

"You're sure that this is the place I own?" Rufus only cocked a brow at him. "Sorry, but mother fuck. I own a service that is going in and disposing of bodies for him? What the hell is the council going to say about this one?"

"I done told them." Sloan stilled. "I didn't have no choice and you know'd it. Beside, that broad that made you take a mate? She said that she'd help you in any way she could. I think she wants this ass bite out of the way as much as you do. And I don't think she's all that king on the fact that he's doing it right under their noses. Did you notice the building over there?"

The building, a nondescript sort of color, was across the street from the house that Fleming was living in. The windows and doors were all glass, but only the select few could see in…just shifters, and only if they had reason to be there. As it was, right now to a human the building simply looked like it was home to some fancy people that liked to look at a trash heap every day. There was even a nice car out front that daily moved to a different location. The Council of Vampires wasn't advertising they were there, but they sure as shit weren't hiding it either.

"What did Delhi say when you told her where the rogue was staying?" He spoke softly and that had Rufus tensing up. Sloan only ever talked like that when he was gearing up something profound. He was more of a shouter than someone who got their underwear in a twist by being all quiet like. "This can't be going over well with them all. I'm assuming you told her that I didn't know."

"I did. And I gave her all we had on what he's been doing, too. She...I just don't understand them people. Anyway, she believed me, if that's what's got your panties in a fart. I mean, what do I look like, a fool?" When Sloan seemed to be considering his answer, Rufus glared. "Bastard. What I meant was, she done gave me clearance to kill him. But so's you know, I am to wait until we have proof but not before. She don't want another Pinwiggle on her hands, but she ain't willing to take any chances this comes on back to bite her in the considerable ass either."

Don Pinwiggle had been a bad seed even before somebody went and made him into a vamp, and the man only got himself into more shit as he grew stronger. Killing humans 'cause he could was just one of many things the man had been up to when he'd been hog tied and brought in. He'd been leaving behind a bloodbath wherever he went, yet it took them right about fifty years before someone got it in their heads to go and find the prick. The only reason he'd been caught at all was that he'd call in to say he'd done it so the clean-up crew could take care of it for him. The body count was nearly a thousand before she'd called in him and Sloan. In two days, not only had they found his lair, they'd been able to bring him in for his death killing too. Rufus shivered when he thought of the way the council took care of their own. It was not a pretty sight. Rufus stayed on their good side so he'd not have his head removed from his body, thank you very fucking much. He looked over at Sloan when he cleared his throat.

"We can't do this on our own, not even with the help of the bums you hired to help us. And we both know that no matter what the council says about us waiting, we're going to end up getting hurt from this. And as much as I don't mind me getting the shit knocked out of me once in a while, I can't have Opal brought in on this. So I asked Blair and the others to come in and help us out. Fleming…Fleming did some damage to Blair's house, so he has a vested interest in this too. We can't watch him all the time and with a new mate…." Sloan looked lost for a second or two, and Rufus wanted to hunt the young pup down and kick her ass. "She really doesn't like me. And when I tried to buy her something, she ranted at me for over an hour about it. Why can't I do this for her when she wants it?"

"Whatcha buy her? Her diamond not big enough or something?" Sloan didn't say anything, and Rufus decided that he didn't like the girl no more. "Want I should have a little talk with her?"

"God, no." Then he laughed. "I didn't buy her a diamond. She…her name is Opal and her sister is Diamond. I should get her…never mind. No, I bought her a building. The one her sister said she was coveting for years. And it has a nice shop in it for her to sell her pretty things in too. I just…shit, I don't know what to do."

A building? Seemed strange even to him, and Rufus knew shit about women. He could lay with one just fine. He'd never had any complaints, but to have one that you wanted to buy shit for? He'd be just as lost. But to turn down a building? He tried to think what to say when Sloan tensed up.

"What is it?"

Sloan nodded to their left, and there were five or six big wolves just standing there. Each of them were a little bit bigger than the next one, and he'd bet his life that the big dark one was this Blair. Rufus had heard nothing but great things about the alpha. Didn't mean he trusted the big wolf, but he did have a better liking for him.

"My new family." As they skirted their way around the buildings toward them, Rufus had a moment of panic. He hated wolves almost as much as he did most humans. This particular group hadn't done a damned thing to him, but he was still a mite on the feared side of them. The biggest one moved into the closest building and came out pulling a shirt over his head. He'd been right as snow about it: the big one was Blair. The others moved in one at a time and did the same thing.

"Rufus, this is my brother-in-law, Blair Henson. His mate is expecting their first child any day now. She's sister to my mate." Rufus took his hand when it was offered and felt the connection like he'd drunk from him. He looked at Sloan. "I don't know why that happens either, so don't ask me. When you meet Quentin and the others, you'll get a better understanding as to why I want to bring these men in. I think it has to do with them killing off Ballard and getting his magic."

He shook hands with all the men that had come with Henson, including the older man, Allen. He thought he knew the man, but he had a hard time remembering shit lately and thought it was his lack of proper rest. When Henson suggested they take over for now, he nodded. Rufus had no idea, but he thought these men were about as trustworthy as Sloan was, and that man he'd do just about anything for.

When he got to his lair, he settled into the bed and closed his eyes. But he heard something right outside his door and tensed. It took him several seconds to realize it was the missus of the house and go to the door. He was glad then that he'd pulled on a pair of his pants. Usually if you came calling for him when the sun was up, you got what you got. She was standing there looking like she was well out of her element. If she was gonna ask him something to do with Sloan, he might well be too.

"I was wondering if you could answer two questions for me. Not counting that one." He frowned. She'd asked him a question? "I don't know how to make my fangs go back. Can you show me?"

Rufus looked at his bed, then back at Opal. He really wanted to like this kid, and there was a time or two when he and Sloan would have shared, but he knew better than to even touch her. Instead he told her he'd meet her in the parlor and turned to get dressed again.

"Damned women folk." But he was right proud she'd asked him.

~~~

Fletcher knew he was being watched. He even had an idea who was doing the watching, but what he didn't expect—and it still surprised him when he thought about it—was that Henson was out there. He had a feeling that he was simply waiting for a mistake, and when Henson found it, Fletcher was as good as dead. And there was no fucking way he was going to let that bastard take him.

"What do you suppose he's looking for? Do you suppose that he thinks I'm going to go out there and just say, 'here I am, kill me now'? Moron." No one answered him, as those in the room with him were all dead. Hell, he figured if he were to go around the house and look, he'd find dead bodies everywhere. He'd gone on a spree last night and now...he looked around the room. This was not what he wanted to see when he'd gotten up this evening. And now that he'd started to remember what had happened, he was surprised that there weren't more dead bodies.

Nineteen...nineteen people had lost their lives because of him being depressed and lonely. He'd been depressed because he'd felt the death of his good friend Marvin. The man had died horribly, and he was reasonably sure it was at the hand of the faerie that had warned them before. So he'd gone out and brought a bunch home with him to mourn his passing.

Fletcher was pretty sure that wasn't right either, the count that he'd come up with to tell the cleaning service. But they'd asked and he had taken a quick inventory of this room only. He'd not left this room, nor had he ventured into the bathroom. Most of them were still bleeding out when he'd woke up about ten hours ago, but he knew that all of them were dead by now. And he was stuck here with them. Fear...fear of what was out there and who was waiting for him had kept him in the house. And now...well, now he had no idea what he was going to do about the bodies or going out to feed.

The cleanup service had said they were running behind when he'd called them the first time. That had been over eight hours ago. And when he'd called them again, they'd told him he was going to have to find another service, as they were no longer cleaning up bodies. Then they'd simply hung up. What the hell had happened in the few hours since they'd done it yesterday? He called back and asked to speak to the manager, and that had made him want to go down there and tear the woman's throat out.

"We are just a cleaning service and no longer dispose of bodies or anything else that does not have to do with cleaning a regular household. I'm sorry, sir, but that part of our business in no longer in operation. The owner was quite displeased that we were...he was unaware of the services we had been providing to you." He asked her who the owner was and if he could speak to him. "No, sir. I'm afraid that's not possible either. He was quite...the crew that was working here is no longer here. I cannot afford to lose my job as well. You'll just have to find other means to take care of this for yourself." And again, he was hung up on.

He thought about going to the place and demanding answers, but he was pretty sure he had them. One of two people owned that business; it was either Henson or Crane. And he'd bet his last dollar it was Henson.

The man had his name on a lot of businesses in the downtown district. There was his business that he let his wife play in, and he was sure that was to keep her out of his hair. Fletcher sneered at the thought of having a woman in the workplace. And then there was the big building across the street that he knew Henson owned and worked from. There were others too, about six all together. The man had his fingers in just about everything.

Again Fletcher thought about how he was nearly always broke, and if not for the fact that he could steal all he wanted when he wanted, he'd never have a thing. Even the house he lived in was one that he'd simply moved into. His magic, what little he had right now, had done a nice job of making the place livable, but it wasn't the place of his dreams. That was something he had a great deal of, big dreams, and someday soon he'd bet he'd have them come to fruition, too.

Fletcher sat at the big desk that came with the house as he contemplated what to do now. He had often wondered if the people who had left the desk had any idea of it's worth. It had taken him a while, but he did now. When things got to be a little tight at one point, he'd tried to sell it, but no one had the means of getting it out of the house without taking down a wall or two. The thing was monstrous.

It was solid oak with maple and cherry trim. The drawer pulls were made of gold and the inlaid desktop was a work of art. The beautifully inlaid wood had been made into a lovely pattern that still amazed him. There just wasn't any way to believe this thing had been completely crafted by hand during the eighteen hundreds. And right now, it was worthless. The blood stains on it would very much lower the value, he thought with a grin. But he had more important things to consider than a desk that was not getting him anything.

*Now what?* He couldn't go out for food. Not that he wasn't full enough now, but he might need a snack later. Fletcher supposed he could go out and kill the wolves milling around his property, but there were so many of them, he was sort of leery about facing them, especially alone like he was now. Without food to replenish himself, he might as well hang a sign around his neck that said, "Free dinner for any of you who want it." Not that he thought they could get the better of him, but why take the chance? Considering what he should, he remembered his meals in the sublevels.

Getting up, he moved to the lower levels, the ones below his lair, to look at the five women and men he had there. Fletcher thought if he were to play for a bit he'd feel a good deal better, so he picked up his blade to lay it on the skin of the first man. The man cringed, and Fletcher felt his mood lift considerably.

"There is no reason for you to act as if you've not been cut by me before. I've taken your leg off, haven't I? And a few other tasty pieces of you." Fletcher licked his lips when he thought of how much he'd enjoyed eating the flesh of his playthings while they had watched. "Do you know that your blood is tastier when you're afraid of me? It is. And there is the added bonus that you're not completely human. Yummy."

He plunged the knife into the man's thigh and listened to him scream around the gag, which he'd had to use because he'd been so whiney. Otherwise he'd enjoyed the way they had begged him before he cut into them. The others had screamed, which was something that he'd expected, but this man was such a baby. As the blood slid down his leg, Fletcher leaned in and licked it. It was so good that he bit into the thick muscle and drank from his vein there. The man, an athlete of some fame, was nearly dead when he pulled away. Fletcher turned to the next plaything, a woman who he'd had for a long while now, nearly three weeks. He wanted to play.

"You would do well not to piss me off again." She nodded but only stared at him. "You can still get around, you know. I mean, it wasn't as if you walked on your hands anyway, now was it?" Having taken off and eaten her hand just last week, he knew that she was weak but far from dead. He thought that in the next few days he'd add her to the body count upstairs if they were still there, and it was beginning to look like they would be. But he shied away from that thought in favor of cheering himself up.

He moved to her pussy and sniffed. She wasn't wet or even aroused a little, not that it mattered to him much. The next man, the one he'd taken a leg from last night, was dead. Good. He'd take care of him later, and it was one less thing he'd have to worry about. He moved to the next woman and man. They had been his prize, but lately, over the past two days, he'd grown quite bored with them too. Who knew that a wolf could be so easily conquered?

"Do you know Henson?" The man nodded. "Me too. Both of them, the older one and the younger. And I have to tell you, they're driving me insane right now. I can't leave my house to feed, and I can't bring in fresh playthings because he and his pack are standing around watching me as if I'm going to do something stupid. I'll have him know that all my plans are well thought out and usually flaw proof."

He played with the couple by flaying open their skin, but not enough to kill them right off. Who knew how long he'd be stuck in here before they got bored and moved on? Then he got the idea to make them have sex with him. He had a few hours to kill before sunrise, so he went to prepare things.

Fletcher had fucked a few men in his life. Not many, but enough to know that he could get off if necessary. But the woman had a nice ass, something he loved more than tits. He pulled them down from the wall and had them shower while he watched. The woman was weak, of course. They all were. But the man was helping her. Fletcher watched as he washed her back and then held her while he washed up her hair. Fletcher felt his dick harden at the thought of the sponge being rolled over his body like that. When he thought them cleaned up, he brought them out to the smallish bedroom he used down here. The man laid the woman on the bed gently, then stood back while Fletcher thought of the perfect way to make this work for him.

"Fuck her." The man backed from the woman. "You heard me. If you can't get it up, then eat her. I just want to watch you and her fuck, and then I'll join you."

"She's another male's mate. I can't do that." Fletcher rolled his eyes and told him to eat her then. "I can't do that. She belongs to another."

"Do you seriously think you're going to get out of here to where he'd find out? Come on, haven't you been paying attention? I kill you all sooner or later. Fuck her. The only people who will know is you and her and, of course, me. And you'll both be dead and I don't particularly give a shit who you fuck. But you'll do it now. I want you to go down on her." The man continued to stand there until Fletcher had to put a knife to his throat and force him to the bed. The motherfucker was taking all the fun out of this for him and no matter what, Fletcher thought, he was as good as dead.

The male got onto the bed, but he didn't look like he was going to do much more than stare at her. Finally, having waited much longer than he wanted, he commanded him to straddle the woman who was laying there and to not move. Then he told the woman to suck the pussy-wolf or he'd kill her. She took the wolf's cock into her mouth so quickly that the male had to hold to the headboard. Fletcher watched her suck him and smiled. Now this was more like it. She looked like she was enjoying herself too, and he could smell her juices.

He felt his cock harden more as he watched them. Getting up on the bed at the bottom, he could see that she was getting wet and settled between her thighs after he stripped off his own clothing. Fletcher was hungry and needy now, and she was going to satisfy both his needs. Her cream was calling to him, and when he spread her, he could see that she was wet. This was how he liked them to be when they weren't screaming: wet or hard and ready to play with him. Burying his face into her pussy, Fletcher fucked her hard with his fingers up her ass and his tongue in her sheath. She came twice while he was still stone hard. He looked up over her plump belly and smiled.

The man was fucking her mouth now, his hips moving fast as his cock disappeared in and out of her mouth. Fletcher moved up behind him and leaned him over her. Fletcher slammed his cock into the male's ass hard as the wolf spilled his cum down her throat. Fletcher came as well and bit deep into his throat as he rode him through another quick climax. But it wasn't enough. Not bothering with sealing up the wounds he'd given the male, he decided that it was his turn to get blown, and tossed the man off the bed.

Fletcher looked down at her body and smiled. Christ, his cock was so hard that he thought about jacking off so he could see himself spray all over her tits before he fucked her. She was bruised and bitten, the scars he'd given her still fresh, but she was fuckable. He wished then that he'd brought the other woman over as well, but he didn't want to move from where he was right now. He had a pussy right where he wanted it now and he needed to fuck something. Flipping her over, he fucked her from behind until she cried out she was coming. Fletcher pounded her harder, taking her to the mattress as he did. He was so close to exploding that he rode her like a dog in heat, his hips moving like the animal he was until his balls tightened to his body and he came again. He didn't care if she got any pleasure from this so long as he got what he wanted. And that was a good fuck.

She came again, this time fingering her own pussy, but he was still hard and needed something else. *Her mouth*, he thought. He'd fuck that mouth of hers until she bled for him. Fletcher rolled her over again and told her to suck him off. She did it with so much suction that he felt his balls

KATHI S. BARTON

tighten almost immediately. He'd give her that much. She could suck rocks from the ground ten feet under.

When he was ready to come again, he pulled from her and reached for his knife. Sliding along his dick, he used the blood to fist himself as he shot his load all over her. As her tongue slid over her bruised and bloodied lips, catching his cum as she cried out, Fletcher moved down her body to settle over her knees.

Fletcher loved the taste of pussy and blood, especially when it was spiked with terror. He cut into her breast and fed from her there while he slid down her blood-slicked body. It was time to fuck this bitch. His cock hardened more at just the thought of doing what he did best.

He moved her legs from under him to get her hips up off the bed. Her pussy was wet now and he opened his mouth to take in the sweet smell of blood and cum. He slid deep into her while holding her legs up to his shoulders. Her tits were moving in time with his fucking, and he smiled. Biting into her thigh, he drank deeply as he came again. He listened to the sound of her heart and thought of two things almost at once. Christ, he was still hard, and she was bleeding out.

He sealed the wounds that he'd made on her thigh and lay over her. The need to change her to keep her as his playmate seemed like a really good idea. Before he could think things all the way through, he filled her with his blood from his wrist while he drank again from her throat. Fletcher knew the exact moment she realized what he was doing.

The begging didn't bother him. He was more than used to that, but what she was saying gave him pause. If what she was saying was true, then he might be able to shift as well. And the thought of being a wolf...well, frankly, it scared the shit out of him. But by the time he thought he should find another female to fuck and let this one die, she was well on her way to being a vampire too. Fletcher lifted his wrist from her mouth to watch the change take her.

Fletcher was so fucked. And when she told him, sobbed to him that she'd rather meet the sun than to be what he was, he picked up his knife and plunged it into her beating heart. She burst into flames before he could move out of the way.

"Solved that for you, didn't I? And now what the hell do I do for fun? Huh? You fucking made it so that not only did I lose three playthings, but you made me have to kill a child of mine." No answer was forthcoming, and by the time he'd jumped off the bed and turned to his other bodies, he realized something too late. They were all dead, and dead meant he had no food until he could get out of his home.

"Mother fuck."

# Chapter 6

Opal watched her sister as she talked on the phone. The woman practically glowed she was so lovely during her pregnancy. She knew that if she got as large as her sister, she'd look like a bloated whale, and feel like it too. A man would run in the opposite direction if she —

"I have nine appointments tomorrow. How the hell do I make nine appointments tomorrow?" She leaned back at her desk and smiled sadly at her. "I had nothing to do with him buying you the building. He asked me what you needed and I just mentioned that you needed a bigger place. I had already set you up to see the house before I spoke to him. I didn't know that he owned the building until you told me. I never thought to look when I set this up."

"But you told him about my appointment." Sapphire nodded. "Did he tell you why he gave it to me? Why he'd give me a building that he already owns when he could just as easily have sold it to me? When I had the money, that is. I mean, he must want something. I have no idea what it might be."

"I'm sure you've given that to him already, Opal." Opal flushed, and Sapphire, of course, laughed at her. "Why are you fighting this? It's what you wanted and you need it more than ever now. Didn't Jade say you had like fifty thousand dollars' worth of orders? You have to have room to make that stuff, right? And as much as I love having you close when you work, that place out there is not going to hold you and all the stuff you need to get started. Where would you store the extra inventory? And you have to admit, having heat and air conditioning will be amazing in the warmer and colder months."

"I was going to make it in my little building, then move it into storage as I completed parts of the whole. It's why I went ahead and took the orders there. I knew that I could make it work from my shop on the property." It would have cost her a fortune too. Paying for storage and having to drive back and forth between her storage unit and her shop was something that she'd counted on but didn't necessarily like. If she decided to use Sloan's building, she'd be able to work and store it all together, as well as have a shop for the extras. It was ideal, yes, but still she didn't want to be beholden to him for anything.

"Opal, this isn't like you to be so impractical. What's really going on here? Is it because he didn't talk to you? Or is it something else?" There was that, but it was not what had her upset. She looked around Sapphire's office, then back at the woman who seemed to not just have it all but knew just what to do with it too.

"He said he'll never love me." Sapphire didn't say anything, and Opal wasn't sure if that was a good thing or not. "I don't love him either. I'm not even sure most of the time I care for him at all. But he's really good at sex. And I suppose that all things considered, that's not a bad way to live. But what of what you and Blair have? I wanted that too someday. But now...well, now I have nothing but a good fuck."

Her face heated when she thought of what he'd done to her in the tiny shed. He'd bitten her pussy and drank deeply from her. She could still feel him suckling at her and her coming a dozen times while he did it. Then he'd stood up and slid his thick cock into her so slowly that she'd wanted to scream at him to take her. But she'd held her tongue until he told her to bite him while he had sex with her.

Her fangs seemed to have a mind of their own most of the time, too. Every time she thought she had a handle on them, the strangest things would make them drop. But the thought of sinking them into Sloan that day had made her gums ache and her canines feel as if they needed to be inside of his skin as much as he was inside of her. She leaned forward and sank her teeth into his pounding pulse, and tasted the difference in him immediately.

He was hers, her wolf and body screamed at her. She wanted to pull him closer to her, have him take her harder, but she was nervous about looking foolish. But he must have known because before she could touch him, he curled his fingers into her hair and pulled her to his body completely as he continued his long, slow strokes.

"Come for me, love." She tried to fight him, but found in the end she wanted this as badly as he did. And when he told her he was coming, her entire body felt as if she were touching a live wire. She would have sworn she felt his cum as it splashed deeply inside of her. Opal looked at Sapphire when she cleared her throat, bringing her back to the present.

"I take it that the sex is better than his manners." Opal nodded and tried not to blush again. "Have you tried talking to him? Telling him what you think about all this? He's usually a reasonable man, and Blair likes him. He can't be all bad if he does. And for the record, Blair said that he's just as confused as you are when it comes to your and his relationship."

"There is no talking to him. He likes things his way, and damn the person who gets in his way. I can't even ask him what he's doing every day because he lies to me. I wonder if he knows I can smell him lying to me." Sapphire said she'd start with that. "Then what? Do I tell him that other than my things, I haven't a clue what to put into the showroom he's suggested that I open in the building? Tell him that other than slap together a few pretty things, I don't have a clue as to what I'm doing? Or do you think he'd want to hear that I still have nightmares about being a failure; that I wait daily for one of those people who bought my jewelry to call me up and tell me that I'm a fraud and that I should be ashamed of myself for trying to pawn something like I make off onto them. I'm sure he'd want to hear about how his mate is as insecure as they come, and is mostly a failure at everything she touches. "

"That's quite enough, young lady." They both turned to see the man in the doorway. Allen was a wonderful man and always seemed to be really happy, but right now he didn't look to be either. He'd been living with them for some time now—since Blair had taken Sapphire as his mate—but Opal had never seen this look on his face before. He was visibly upset.

"I'm sorry you had to hear that." Allen nodded and looked to his right. Their grandmother walked into the office then, and both of them stood up. She kissed Opal first, then Sapphire.

"You've been complaining, I guess." Opal looked at Allen when he nodded. "I see. Are things just going too nicely for you then? Or do you like being a whiney little brat? This is not like you at all, young lady. And frankly, I'm having a very difficult time trying to figure out why you'd think that you're a failure."

"I'm neither whiney nor a brat, thank you. I have a mate that I don't like who is trying to buy his way into my heart. I won't have it." As soon as she said it, Opal knew it for the lie it was. "I don't want him to be my mate. I just want to be left alone to do what I want, when I want."

"You're lying to yourself then, even if you think half of that is true. I'm thinking you've just not thought about loving him, so you believe it not to be right. But if you ask me, I think you're as much in love with him as he is with you." Opal shook her head, but her grandmother wasn't having it. "Think about it. And while you do, stop complaining about the building he already owned before he met you and move out of that tiny little place you work in. My granddaughters are making something of themselves, and you're holding things up. Don't you want to succeed?"

"He turned it over to me and I feel like he bought me off." She looked at Sapphire, who appeared shocked. "It's just the way I feel. I can't help but think that he wants me in his bed, and figured I'd fall over him when he gave me what I wanted."

"You don't believe that any more than I do. The man is besotted with you, and more than that, he did something nice for you, and you're being too much of a stubborn baby to let him help you. What is wrong with you that you can't take something someone wants you to have? It still belongs to you." Her grandmother sat down and eyed her with such a look that Opal squirmed. "You do love him, don't you, child? And you're just too much like him to admit it. Not even to yourself."

Opal didn't love him. She liked him well enough, she supposed, most of the time, but he was overbearing and too full of himself for her to even think of loving him. It was simply the satisfaction of all the sex she was having that her grandmother could see. That was it, and not love. Sloan was a man who fell in love with women that would hang on his every word, and not someone who was too shy to tell him that she loved the building but was afraid. Instead of digging too deeply into her feelings, she changed the subject to something else that was bothering her.

"What am I supposed to do with the rest of the building? He said I should have a shop. A shop. What do I do with a shop?" She looked at her grandmother, who smiled at her. "You think I can do this? I don't have any idea what kind of things people would buy or how much they'd pay."

"You should talk to your sister, Jade. She can help you put some stuff in that front window. Did you see what she's done to the outside of the greenhouse? I nearly told her to pack it up so I could put it out here. But she was too busy." Opal told her grandmother that she'd designed that before she could think that Jade should have the credit. It had been her idea to decorate. She'd only given her what she thought would go well together. "And here you are worried about filling your own windows. My goodness, child, get started. Any and all of us would help you. I might even be talked into ringing up a few customers just to have some fun. And I know that I'd be a good customer too."

Started? And how the hell was she supposed to afford that too? Opal left them a little while later, no closer to figuring out what to do than before. When she drove by the building, her building, she stopped, and before she could change her mind, got out of her car and went inside. Again she was struck by the vastness of the first floor, and wandered around trying to imagine it all filled with small, special things that people would buy.

*Are you close to Blair's building?* She was startled out of thoughts of building a large display of candles in her mind when Sloan touched her mind. *I need you to come to me if you can. I need...I've been hurt. Not badly, but enough that I would like to drink from you. And maybe a little loving too.*

*Hush. I'm on my way.* She locked up the building and was crossing the street when she saw Blair. He had blood on his shirt and he was watching the street. When he saw her, she thought he looked relieved, and that made her move a little faster. By the time they were riding up the elevator, Opal was frantic with worry. There was a great deal of blood, not just on his shirt but his pants as well. He told her it wasn't his but Sloan's and Rufus's. Both of them had been hurt while protecting him.

She saw Sloan lying on the couch that was in Blair's office. The thought of turning around and running made her pause in mid-step, but then he looked at her. There was something there, pain for sure, but something that made her stare at him until he put out his hand. Opal heard the door close behind her and knew that Blair had left them. She walked to the couch and sat down on her knees beside him as he held her hand.

"What happened?" She lifted the blood-soaked towel and looked at the claw marks along his belly. The sight of his wounds nearly made her belly turn up, but she recovered when he put his hand on her cheek. She felt the sticky blood that had been on his fingers and the coldness of his touch. "You're too weak, aren't you? Why didn't you just tell me that you needed me to come to where you were instead of coming here?"

"The sun was coming up and I couldn't go to cover by myself. Blair thought he'd keep me safe here until I could get well enough to travel." Sloan shifted slightly on the couch, and she could see the pain on his face. "We were ambushed. I was thinking of this pretty little woman that I had the most incredible sex with this morning, and Fletcher came around the corner and hit me." Her temper flared, and he laughed.

"Well, if you had gotten what you needed from her, why are you still hurt?" She started to stand, but he held her to him. "I don't want to be near you right now. I have an uncontrolled urge to hit you."

"I was talking about you, Opal. This morning in your little office nearly made me want to hunt you down and taste you that way again. It...well, thoughts of you screaming out my name again had me sort of distracted." He kissed her gently on the mouth. "Christ, do you have any idea how much I enjoyed that? Drinking from you while your pussy gushed out your cream? I wish I could do it again and again." Her body heated and she shifted on her knees to try and relieve the sudden pressure. When Sloan moaned, she wanted to open her legs and give herself to him, but he was hurt and needed her.

"You should pay attention to your surroundings and you'd not be cut up like this." He nodded, and she felt tears start to fall. "I could feel your hurt when I heard from you. I can only assume that you'd blocked me from feeling you before. I...you terrified me when you asked for me to come here. I thought...I don't know what I thought, but I was afraid."

"You are the most beautiful creature I've ever seen." He kissed the tear that was falling on her cheek. Then he kissed her mouth. She felt his cold lips move along her throat before he lifted his head and looked at her. "I have to ask you something before I drink from you. And I want you to think about your answer before you say it. All right?"

"Feed first. Right now you're too weak to talk about anything. Just do it." He shook his head. Fear made her sharper than she'd meant to be. "Why the hell not? You called me here, didn't you?"

"I did. I wish that I hadn't, but I did." She sat back on her heels as her heart shattered in her chest. She could hardly breathe around the pain of it. And as she started to stand up to leave, he continued. "If you were not to feed me I would die. You'd live because of your being a wolf, but then you'd be rid of me. And we both know you want that more than anything. But you're going to be well cared for, even when I die. I have taken the liberty of putting your name alongside of mine on all my accounts in the event that I do perish. I wouldn't blame you for leaving me here, but when I was bleeding out, all I could think about was how much I dearly love you."

"You don't mean that. You don't love me at all. You're just afraid and I'm here. You don't have to lie to me. You don't love me." He nodded and held her hand. "Sloan, this is just stupid. Feed so we can get you home and into your lair."

"No. I don't think that's a good idea. Because as much as I'd like to tell you that I'm only saying these things to you to guilt you into saying you love me too, I know that you don't. And I no longer want to make you stay with me when this is an easy out for you. You and I would be the only ones that would ever know. And Blair already thinks that I'm going to die anyway. I lost a great deal of blood back there."

"Why are you doing this? Why are you saying these things right now, Sloan? You think so little of me that you think I could let you die? You think that—" He cut her off with his mouth. It was hungry and full of need, but before she could let him bite her, he was pulling back and staring at her. "I can't do this. You have to know that this isn't right."

He nodded and closed his eyes. As soon as she stood up, she went to the door and looked back at him. He expected her to leave him. He really expected her to simply leave him to die. And why not? She was just as her grandmother said, a whiney brat who didn't know a good thing when she had it. She turned the lock, and he opened his eyes to look at her.

"I'm going to heal you, but I have rules first, all right? You feed from me and I want to ride you. I've never done that before, and I'd very much like to try it if you're up to it." He watched her walk to him as she kicked off her shoes. "I think that's only fair, don't you? I give you my blood and I get to come all over your cock."

"Ride me how?" She knew that he'd understood her and hoped that he'd just say it, but he was waiting on her. Opal swallowed hard as she pulled her blouse up and over her head. He didn't say anything as she took off the rest of her clothing except the panties and bra she'd bought for herself while she'd been in Paris. She knew that he liked them, and decided right then and there to get more of the lacy, pretty things.

"As in you have your cock deep inside of me and I sit on you while taking my own pleasure. I'll play with my nipples too, make them ache to be suckled by you. Will you do that for me, Sloan? Suckle at my breast while I ride your cock?" He nodded and didn't move when she stood in front of him. "You'll have to help me. I have no idea how to make this work. And you should know something else…I'm afraid. I'm terrified that I'll disappoint you."

"Never. You could never disappoint me in anything you do. Right now I'd like to do just what you want, but I'm afraid I don't have enough blood in me to get hard right now." She shivered when she remembered his wound. "I can…will you let me feed from your wrist first? I won't ask you to seal the wounds with your mouth because I know that's asking a lot. But you can—"

"Tell me how to do it." He stared at her, and she dropped to her knees. "Do I just hold you together and seal it shut like I do at your neck?"

Lifting the padding, she closed her eyes as he helped her pull the two large wounds together. She ran her tongue over the first one, the smaller of the two, before she looked at him. His face was in pain and she asked him if he was hurting.

"I am. But not from what you're doing. I want to feel you lick my cock that way as soon as I'm hard. I want to fuck you down the back of your throat until I fill you." She sealed the other wound quickly. Then he took her throat. His bite was savage, but she held him to her. She nearly came when he moaned. There was something so primal, so erotic to have him take her so hard. She felt her pussy soak her panties and touched her clit while he fed. He tore his mouth from her and looked at her.

"Ride me." She moved over him, and he tore her panties from her body. As soon as he was cradled in her hips, his hands grabbed her hips and he pulled her down over him. Neither of them moved for several seconds. He not only filled her but he consumed her with his look too. Then he sat up and took her nipple into his mouth and bit her again. Opal came, screaming his name as he rolled her to the floor and took her hard.

"Next time." She looked up at him as she pulled her hips up and he pounded into her. "Next time I have you naked I'm going to let you ride me until your heart's content. But right now, I need to fuck you until neither of us can move. Christ, baby, I love you."

Sloan kissed her again. He wasn't holding back now but showing her with his mouth and body just how much he wanted her, how much he loved her. When she came again, her body seemed to fuse with his as he came with her. When he bit her this time, sinking his fangs into her pulse, she felt her love for him pour from her every pore. Opal screamed again when he brought her to a blinding climax by entering her mind and him showing her what she was making him feel. Opal let the darkness slide over her as she held her secret for just a little while longer as she came again. Her body seemed not to be able to take so much emotion and pleasure. Opal was in love with her mate.

~~~

Fletcher had to find a place to lay low. He was hurting, and not just a little either. He looked down at his broken arm and the blood that dripped from his neck. That fucking bastard had clawed him. How the hell was he supposed to know that Crane was able to shift like that? Mother cock sucker, he was hurting.

He'd gotten out of his house before sun up. Fletcher hadn't, of course, had a chance to feed when he'd come upon the two men, Crane and Rufus, standing there talking. Crane had seen him at the last second, but Rufus didn't until the man turned to him. He'd been so panicky to see Henson coming out of the building too that he'd reacted before thinking that three-on-one were odds not in his favor. But before he could lash out and kill any of them, Crane had shifted so quickly that it had startled Fletcher for a few seconds. And that was all it had taken for him to get the living shit beat out of him. Lucky for him, when Crane had gone down after he shifted, Henson had moved to help him rather than chase after him. Rufus had been hurt too, but Fletcher doubted that it was as badly as he'd been hurt.

The building that he moved into was close to his own home, but he knew that if he went there, he was as good as dead. First of all, there was no food for him; and secondly, that would be the first place they looked. He was sure that Rufus was hot on the trail to get there and look him up. Fletcher was worried that Henson could find him anyway, but so long as he had to attend to Crane, it might buy him some time to heal. Fat chance.

Fletcher was weak from blood loss, and worse yet, he'd been broken up too. He needed to feed or he'd die. But his clothing was a mess, so going to find food was out, and he'd never had a cell phone so he couldn't even call anyone to come to his aid. Not that he knew anyone that wouldn't just as soon stake him than help him. Marvin had been his only friend in that respect, and he was dead now.

The building was completely devoid of all life, including that of humans. If he wasn't hurting so badly, he might think that was a good thing, but right now, he needed something or someone to help. He had no idea what he was going to do, but he had to do something. Fletcher laid down in the darkest corner of the basement he could find and looked down at his body. Fuck.

Not only was his arm nearly shattered, but two of his fingers were missing as well. He could heal himself if he found someone to feed him, but there was no way for him to grow parts back. He mourned the loss of his digits as he continued his inventory. Fletcher knew that his face had suffered as well, and moaned over the loss of what he thought of as his best feature. Closing his eyes one at a time, he could see that while his face was hurting, he could still see. He looked down at his legs.

Rufus had gotten in on that. Fletcher knew that he'd have to make him pay, but he had to get the wounds taken care of first. The large gash at his groin had barely missed his main artery, but he was still bleeding like he'd cut it open. The tourniquet was soaked through with his blood, but now that he was no longer moving, it wasn't pouring from him. He'd been terrified when he'd seen that opened bleeding wound, and thought for sure he was dead.

"Slimy douche canoe." Fletcher felt somewhat better as he shouted out names to the men who had hurt him. He tried to think around the pain for more names to call the three men, and started making things up. "Captain idiotic rectum cock knob. Dicknosed sphincter waffle goblin." Laughing despite the pain, he thought one more should do it. "Pompous bitch turd fuck nut lazy crotch muffin."

Fletcher felt his body begin to shut down and wondered briefly if he'd wake up at sunset, or even if he wanted to. The pain was incredible and he reached out for any human he could find. As he drifted off, he heard someone come near him, but was too weak to fight them if they came to cause him harm. Just as the old man walked up to him and put his finger at his throat to no doubt check for a pulse, Fletcher used the last of his strength to grab the man and bring him to his mouth. The taint of drugs and sickness nearly had him pull away, but he needed the nourishment more than he liked to think about. Instead of letting the man go when he'd had enough, Fletcher drank until he felt like he couldn't hold any more, then let himself slip away. The man's last breath was all Fletcher heard before the sun pulled him under.

# Chapter 7

Ruby was exhausted. Not only had she put in a sixteen-hour shift, she'd been on her feet for most of that. And the body count was continuing to grow from the accident that had taken more lives than it hadn't, but now it was starting to slow and she needed a break. She'd finally had to tell the nurses that she was too hungry, and was going to see about getting something to eat. But as she entered the small doctor's lounge, she felt the vampire enter behind her. Ruby turned slowly and looked at the handsome yet blood-covered man.

"I'm on break." He nodded and stood there. "Do you know who I am? If you do, you're well aware that I'm sister to the alpha bitch. I'm not going to go down easily if that's what you think. I'm a wolf of her own right."

"Yeah, I can see that. And I know who you are. You be the sister to Sloan's mate. And I comed here to see if you could help me out. I tried to fix it myself, but I can't." He lifted the coat he'd had draped over his arm, and she could see the rod sticking out of his arm. "I think it might be inside of a bone or something. Darn near passed out when I worked it to death. I might be needing to...do you think you can fix me up?"

She moved to help him to one of the unused cubicles and pulled the coat off completely. The rod, about nine inches long, was protruding from both the top and bottom of his arm just below the elbow. He looked like he was in a great deal of pain too. Her heart went out to the man, because every time she touched his arm or the rod, he'd simply inhale sharply but said nothing.

"I can offer you something to ease it, but I don't think it'll work. I've got some things here I can use to help you, but again, I don't think it will do you much good." He shook his head and watched her closely. "I'll help you, but you need to give me something in return."

"Return for help? Boy, you sure you ain't related to Sloan by blood? Never seen a man that could bargain you to near ruin if he wanted you to do something." He eyed her hard. "I'm not going to kill anybody for you. I done seen the way that there doctor talked to you, acting like he was so much smarter. He ain't, you know. Dumb as a box of nuts and bolts if you asked me. Durn near went to him and tore his throat out. Might still do that, too, if'n he don't change his music."

"Thank you very much. But please don't kill him just yet. I'd have to cover his shift, and even though he doesn't do all that much, it's better than me doing it all by myself. I think he's a moron as well." Ruby stepped back before she decided to help him anyway and put out her hand. "Do we have a deal? Or do I go find Nuts and Bolts and let him work on you?"

She knew he was very weak, terribly so. But she held her ground. It was everything she could do not to simply give in. But a perfect opportunity had been handed to her, and this might be her only chance to get at least part of what she'd been thinking of for years.

"I'll do it." She smiled at him and he looked at her suspiciously. "You don't want me touching you. We'll have a connection that won't be broked up by washing your hands with that handisizer."

It took her a moment to realize that he meant hand sanitizer but nodded anyway. But in the end he took her offered hand. She studied his arms for several minutes before she told him what had to happen. Making small talk first to sort of relax him, she asked who else might have been hurt.

"That alpha, but he's not hurt much. A bump on the head, maybe. Me and Sloan got the worst of it, but Blair, he held his own. Was taking care of Sloan when I had to chase down Fleming." He winced twice when she touched him too hard. "I don't want you to be offended, but if'n you keep that up, I'm not going to be all that pleasant to be around. I ain't used to being on my best behavior around womenfolk like you, and I might say some words you ain't never heard before."

"I live with a household full of women. I'm pretty sure whatever you have to say, I've heard it before. And working in the emergency room, people tend to say what they think there as well. But I want you to know that I have to re-break the bone. It's fused around the rod, and that's the only way I can think to get it out." He nodded and told her to go for it. "You'll need blood. I can get you a few bags if you tell me what—"

"Can't. I don't...I can't drink from no Baggie. I won't even go into what that shit tastes like when you wrap it up all pretty like." He shivered and stared at her before looking away. "You just fix me up and I'll find me something. But I gotta pull the darkness around us before you start. There are a few out there that would come to running when I start yelling, and I'd just as soon they didn't find me like this."

"I want you to bite me." He shook his head. "It's what I want in the deal. And I want to have a real climax when you do it. It's what I'm going to trade you for, for fixing your arm."

"Real? What do you mean, real? You ain't had a man so you can't have had one yet." He glared. "Sloan put you up to this to see if I'd do it. Damn that man to hell and back. And here I was thinking he'd been too hurt to do more'n let his mate fix him up. Well, you tell him that I ain't like that. That I ain't going to—"

"No. No, you misunderstood me. I need to have a real climax, not one I manufacture for myself. I have toys that I use, you see, and I just know that there is more to it than the little bit of satisfaction I get when I use them. And since I never plan on having a mate—I've taken precautions for that—I want to see what the difference is. And I'm sure there is a difference. There is, right?" Rufus started to shake his head even before she was done. "You can make me come without using your body, can't you? I know you can. You're just being stubborn now."

"Maybe I am, but that don't mean...damn it, woman. And as for giving you a climax? I can, but I ain't gonna. What the hell is wrong with you that you...what the fuck is a toy? You mean one of those vibrating dicks? You use one of them?" She nodded and flushed again. "You know a man can eat you right up and it not be sex? Go and find you a nice man to have some pussy eating with you. You'd like that real fine. And I'm betting it'll be a damned sight better than that vibrating dick you been using. Damn it...double damn and shit fire."

"No, I don't want to have oral sex with a man. I don't want a stranger's scent on me." He told her she'd have his scent and she nodded. "I know. I'm hoping that…with me helping you and you needing my blood, no one will be the wiser as to what I've done. My family won't know what we did about me coming, only that you bit me. Not that I wanted you hurt, but I thought I'd just be one of your donors and get you to help me this way. Any vampire would have been okay, but I know you, sort of, so it's okay."

Rufus stared at her again. She wanted to squirm but she only looked him in the eye. When he finally nodded, she did as well. Suddenly she was embarrassed to the point that she could no longer look him in the face.

"We can't be doing this here." She nearly cried with relief. "If you're set on this, we have to go somewhere we can have some privacy. When you come like you want, I want to be able to make it worth your while. And this here place is not where I'd like to hear you scream. Cause, darling, you are going to scream."

She nodded once and was suddenly sitting on a big bed with him. Ruby looked around the room, then back at him. This was his room, and he'd brought her here to let her come and for her to help him. Ruby wanted to tell him there wasn't going to be actual intercourse, but was afraid he'd change his mind so she looked at his arm.

It took her nearly an hour to get the rod free. She was drenched in sweat by the time it had come out, and he'd been cursing like a sailor on leave nearly the entire time. When he slipped away at one point, she'd broken another smaller bone and had the rod out before he opened his eyes. She taped the ends of the wound closed so that he'd not scar. Ruby did what she needed while he lay there looking at her. To say she was uncomfortable would have been a gross understatement. But instead of begging him to stop staring at her, she tried her best to ignore him. At some point, however, she had a feeling he'd changed his mind.

Ruby was cleaning up when he spoke again. "I ain't gonna to do this, honey. I can't be taking your blood, and making you have your first climax with a man isn't really anything I wanna do either. I'm real sorry. But you have to understand that this is the job of your mate, and I'd be taking something that belonged to him."

"I didn't think you would." As she cleaned up the room, stuffing the bloodied rags and gauze into the bag she'd had out at the hospital, she tried not to think what she'd just done. While she never thought of herself as all that much, being turned down by a vampire who needed her was more painful than she'd thought it would be. Instead of giving into the tears that seemed right on the surface, Ruby tried to think if there was anyone else that she knew who would do this for her. When she was ready to go, she looked at him and smiled.

"You gonna give up this notion? Or you gonna go out and find the first vampire you can see and have him take over where I didn't want to step?" She shrugged and moved to the door. "I wish you'd give this up. You could get hurt, or even worse, you could get yourself killed off. What the hell would your family do with that on their heads if'n you did that? Just give up this foolish idea and we'll be friends. Deal?"

"If you'd take me back to the hospital again, I can finish up my shift. I know that if I lay these things out in the sun, your blood will disappear, right?" He nodded but didn't move. "I'll make sure I do that before I toss them out. And no one will know that I helped you either. I understand that a wounded vampire can be prey to all sorts of problems."

"You didn't answer me." She only stared at him. "You're gonna do this without me helping you, ain't you? You're going to go on ahead and find you somebody that'll bite you, might even tear your throat out, just so's you have a real climax. What if you find yourself a man like Fleming? What if he wants more than just a quick climax and he takes what you ain't offering?"

"I'll be fine, Rufus. Believe it or not, I've given this a great deal of thought. And I'm not nearly as stupid as some people think that I am. This is no longer any of your concern." Ruby looked at him and tried to hide the fact that she was dying inside. He'd turned her down was all she could think about. "I'd like to leave now."

When he stood up, she waited for him to wrap his arm around her to take her back. It had happened so quickly before that she'd been startled. But now she was prepared. She wondered about the few pieces of equipment that had come with them but didn't want to ask him. Her heart was breaking and she wanted gone. But when he pulled her to his body, she was still and her mind shut down.

"I'm gonna do this, but you know you're signing my death certificate, don't you?" She shook her head. "I'm supposing you have a plan for that, too? You do have it all worked out in that pretty little head of your'n, don't you? Well, I'm hoping so, for both our sakes."

"I'll tell them you needed blood and I gave it to you." He nodded and turned her in his arms. He was strong even with all the blood he'd lost, and she had a slight moment of panic. But he wrapped his arm around her waist and pulled her body flush with his. His cock was there, but he wasn't hard like she'd expected. Before she could ask if he was hurt there too, he spoke.

"I can't get hard, but you don't need me to be for this." She moaned when he licked her throat. "Christ, I forgot you're a wolf. Drinking from you is going to give me the energy I need right now. I done went and forgot that for a minute. Do you know what your blood does for me?"

"No." He licked her again, and she had to press her legs together to try to give her heating pussy some relief. He told her to stop. Then he cupped her ass and brought her tighter to him. Ruby had to hang onto him or fall. Her entire body was on fire.

"Your arousal helps me." He licked her again before he grazed his fangs over her pounding pulse. "I need more than I thought. You okay with me taking a sip or two more?"

Before she could form a thought, not even sure what it might have been, he bit her. His fangs sank deep and she cried out a release. She nearly pulled away from him, disappointed that the vibrator had given her more, when he cupped her breast, bra and all. His cock began to fill between them and she rocked back into him. He moaned again and put his hand between them and cupped her pussy while she fed him.

*Come for me.* His command had her coming hard. His fingers dug deep into her folds, and he set her off again when his fingers touched her clit. The second and third time he told her to come, she cried out and held his hand to her while he gave her another brief yet satisfying climax. He lifted his head from her throat, and she could see his beast. For whatever insane reason she had, Ruby wasn't afraid of him. But he looked at her as if he could have devoured her without a single thought.

He didn't kiss her, and as badly as she wanted it, she knew that it would be too much for her. When he lifted her up, her legs wrapped around his hips and then the wall was at her back. The moment she was fully against it, he started rocking into her with punches of his cock, his shaft, so hard now all she could think about was him filling her with it. As she built even higher, her body as tightly strung as a bow, he lifted his head and looked at her again. He looked hungry, and she wanted to feed him as badly as he looked like he wanted to feast on her.

"Scream for me when you come. I want to drink deeply from you when you do, and you'll heal me." She nodded, knowing that no matter what, she'd give him whatever he needed. This time when he suckled at her throat, she felt his hand slide into the back of her pants, and he pressed against her tight hole. It was so unexpected yet so wonderfully amazing that she cried out when he pressed his finger into her.

Her climax grabbed her tightly around her body and then tore from her. She couldn't have held back her scream if her very life depended on it. As she drew in a breath to come a second time, he rocked against her clit and she came three more times. Even as her body begged her to stop—it was too weak to go again—Rufus pulled away and helped her to the chair.

"Christ, you can make a man forget about promises." She reached for him again, his thick cock straining against the front of his pants. He took a step back and put this hand over himself. "You touch me like I can see you wanna and we're both gonna be fucked. You with my cock and your family will kill me. I'll take care of this later. Right now...well, did you get what you wanted? Did you enjoy that more'n that vibrating dick?"

"That was amazing." He grinned at her and she smiled back. "Do you make women want to swoon when you fuck them? Is it always like that with you?"

"Nope, better when we both are nekked and rolling in a big bed fucking. And so's you know, I like to have my women tied up and panting for me too. I don't do vanilla sex that often, but I'd do it with you right quick if I wasn't afraid of dying because of it." He looked her over and she felt as if he was truly seeing her as naked as the day she'd been born. "Course, you keep looking at me like that and I'll forget that sister and alpha of your'n. I might even go so far as to fuck that no doubt pretty pussy of your'n too."

Ruby wasn't sure if she should believe him about being better in the bed. But the rest of what he'd said had her heating up. When he asked her if she was satisfied, she smiled at him and was delighted to see him blush. Ruby thought that if sex could be better with him, she wasn't sure she wanted any more. Her entire being was still vibrating with her climaxes.

"I'm going to take you back now," he told her with a sort of gruff voice. "If'n you'd do me a big favor and not lean too hard into me, I'll get you there still intact."

Nodding once, she was suddenly standing in the small cubical she'd first taken him to. And she was alone. It was probably better that way. She had embarrassed him as much as he had her, and she might need a few days, or months, to be able to look him in the eye again.

Ruby sat on the bed and tried to think if she'd ever felt this wonderful before. She decided that she hadn't, and smiled as she made her way to the cafeteria. Suddenly she wasn't just hungry but starved, and she also needed something to drink. Ruby decided that her vibrator just wasn't going to cut it any longer and tried to think how much bigger she should go. Her body was still humming an hour later when she entered the trauma unit again.

~~~

Sloan watched Opal sleep. She was resting so deeply that he'd checked her breathing three times before he finally laid down beside her. He felt Rufus touch his mind and nearly told him to leave them alone when he remembered that he, too, had been hurt.

*I'm going to be fine,* he said in way of greeting. *But I got me something to confess. You're not going to like it one little bit and might even leave that cozy little bed you got yourself there and come after me. So's I'm telling you now before you find out afore hand.*

*What have you done?* Sloan felt his body tense up knowing that if he said confess rather than just tell him, it was going to be bad. *Rufus?*

*I done went and saw that Gem you been telling me about. The one that's a doc? She fixed me up right good. Then I bit her. And made her come.* Sloan stood up and reached for the man to see where he was. *Don't come here. I done had to find me a safe-like place to rest, and you coming here and killing me is just going to piss me off. And I feel too good for you to fuck me up like that. I didn't hurt her.*

*You bit into my sister-in-law? An innocent? Do you have any idea what the penalty is for that? Not to mention what Blair and the...holy Christ, Sapphire is going to fucking kill you. And right now, I'm inclined to help her do it.* Sloan tried to think how he could save his friend, but he could only think how her family was going to murder them both, simply because they were both vampires. *Rufus, what the hell were you thinking? And for that matter, what was Ruby thinking? You two aren't mates, are you?*

*Hell no, we ain't mates. Christ, and I didn't have sex with her. She wanted to come and I helped her. Did you know them there vibrating dicks don't really satisfy like a man will? And I told her, I told her a few times she could have a man go on down on her, but she said she didn't want his scent.* Sloan started to point out that she had his now, but Rufus continued. *She kinda tricked me into it. Said she'd help me if'n I traded her. I'm thinking to myself, 'Rufus, man, you're so going to regret this' and damned if I didn't tell it like it was. It was more'n I bargained for, even when I helped out your missus, but then she only had a few hundred questions. Even though she only said it was two. But I think that I —*

*Rufus.* Sloan tried to think when he'd been more frustrated with the man and couldn't think beyond what he'd just said. *You helped Opal out? When was this? You know what, I don't think I want to get into that with you right now. Where did you have this nonsexual encounter with Ruby?*

*My bedroom.* Sloan wanted to bang his head against the wall. They'd been doing this in his house. In the room he had given Rufus when he'd purchased the house. *She would've brought the house down had we did it at her work. That girl has a set of lungs on her.*

Sloan said his name again to shut him up. *What did you do to her? And I mean, exactly what did you do to her?*

*I fed from her. She offered up her own vein for that. And the deal was, she'd take the pike out of my arm and I'd help her with something. I didn't know what I agreed to until it was done too late. I told her she was more related to you than she thought. Didn't 'spect that from her, her being all quiet and all. She's slick like that.* Sloan was going to kill them both. *Then when she said why she needed me, I couldn't turn her down. Did you know that she's taken precautions so her mate never finds her? How does one get something like that done? I'd be willing to pay just about anything for me not to be a sap like you are right about now.*

Sloan looked at the bed and into the dark brown eyes of Opal. The woman was simply the most gorgeous thing he'd ever seen. And when Rufus laughed, he had to turn from her or close out his friend and take her again and again.

*You should know that I'm going to tell Opal. And she'll more than likely hunt you down before any of them. I'm telling you this because if you have a desire to leave the country, now would be a good time to do so.* Rufus said he was staying. *Then heaven help you. They are going to be after your ass in no time.*

*She doctored me right up, you know. Did it without a single hesitation as to what I am and what I might have done to get that way. She's a good kid.* Sloan hoped she was understanding too, and thought about him having a conversation with Blair and decided that he'd rather be dead. *Sloan, she's not hurt in any way. I'm only telling you so's you know when you smell her on me. And you will. But she's planning on telling everybody she helped me out and I needed to feed. Which is true enough. I wasn't going to make it without her help.*

Sloan looked back at Opal, who reached for him. He told Rufus he had to go and pulled Opal into his arms. She laughed when he simply held her.

"She told me." He lifted her chin up. "I already spoke to Ruby and she told me what happened. She said to tell you, but I'm guessing that Rufus already did."

"He did. Are you upset? I can kill him if you want. I'd rather see him dead than anyone in your family hurt. And while I think the world of my friend, I'm terrified of Sapphire and the rest of them, but mostly her."

"No. It's fine. Ruby has been planning something like this for years, I think. She told me a few weeks ago. And Sapphire is a sweetheart so long as you're up front and honest with her. She's only seeing to us, as she has always felt she should." She stretched over him and he rocked into her heat. When she moved up and over his lap, he decided that being a sap, as Rufus called him, wasn't all that bad.

"Can I ride you now? You said that the next time you had me naked I could ride you. And in the event you didn't notice, I'm very naked." He nodded but she was way ahead of him, pulling the sheet off her so that she was now showing him how gloriously naked she was. "I think that if Rufus had made love to her like you do me, she'd never leave the bedroom again. As it was, he nearly took her head off with her enjoyment. I'm thinking I'd very much like to see if I can do that for you. Make your head explode in pleasure."

"He said she won't tell. Will she?" He forgot to listen for her answer when Opal sat up and he helped her take his cock into her. "Christ, you're so wet. And I think if you keep this up, not only will my head explode but my cock will empty into you before you get any pleasure at all."

Her ride was slow at first. As much as he wanted to guide her, he also didn't want to have her stopping anytime soon. So he held off from touching her, knowing the moment he did he was going to roll her to her back and take her hard. When she threw back her head, rolling her nipples between her fingers, Sloan leaned up and took one of the pert tips into his mouth and nibbled. She curled her fingers into his hair and held him to her as her ride grew harder, faster until he knew she was close. When he bit her, sinking his fangs deep into her, and nursed, her movements took on a very desperate gait.

"I want to fuck you." She shook her head, and he pulled her harder down over him. "Baby, I need to come too. Let me pound that pretty pussy of yours."

She leaned forward, and he let her have his throat. He wanted to feel her bite him while he took her, and rolled her to her back anyway. Even as she drank from him, he took her deeper than he'd ever done before, and she tightened around him before he could reach his own peak. Her coming had him taking her harder even as he took her wrist to his mouth. Sloan felt as if he'd finally come home when he released, her body holding his heart along with his body. Her being didn't just accept him but seemed to need him as much as he did her, and Sloan needed her very much. Sloan was in love with his mate.

Falling atop her, he tried to catch his breath. Christ, she was amazing. He lifted his head to tell her again how much he loved her. But the tears falling down her cheeks had him kissing her gently. Sloan felt his heart, so freshly mended with his realization that he loved her, tear into tiny bits.

"What is it? Have I hurt you?" He started to pull away from her when she tightened her legs and held him. "Opal, what is it, honey?"

"I love you." He felt as if he had just won the lotto and nearly cried out with joy, but he stilled when she continued. "I didn't want to. I know that you'll tire of me and someday leave me, but I've fallen in love with you and I don't know what to do. I just…I never wanted anyone to love me, never wanted to be hurt by love. And now, now I'm in love with you."

Sloan held her. He had no idea what he could to do prove to her how much he honestly loved her, so he held her to his body. When she was relaxed, her body claimed in sleep, he held her still. Sloan knew for as long as he lived he'd make sure she knew daily how much he loved her. And he'd try to show her that she could love him without any fear of him leaving or tiring of her.

# Chapter 8

Fletcher woke slowly. He had a hard time thinking where he was, and when he stretched out, the burning pain of the sun touching his bare skin made it all come rushing back. Opening his eyes, he looked down at the dead man that lay over him. Tossing him away, Fletcher took a quick inventory of his body.

His arm was mending but still pained him terribly. He knew that breaks like he'd had would take a few more feedings to heal completely, so that didn't worry him overly much. His belly was still tender as well, but he thought he could stand now if necessary. But there would be no more running from crazed shifters anytime soon. Using the wall as support, Fletcher made his way to a standing position only to fall back again. His legs simply would not hold his weight. It took him nearly an hour of breathing slowly and moving even more slowly for him to be able to move back deeper into the building so he wouldn't burn before the sun completely went down. He would have to rest before he could try to move out again, and feed. And try as hard as he could, no other humans came to him.

It took him nearly all his strength and over three hours before he felt as if he could move on his own. The loss of his fingers bothered him, and he hoped that Sloan was sick on them, assuming he was the one who had bitten him. Things were a blur now that he'd had time to think. And he was pretty sure that he'd killed one, maybe even as many as two of his attackers before it was all done. He was nearly to his house when he realized that something was off about the scene in front of him. He just stared at the house that he'd been living in for so long, as if it were a surreal painting that he just didn't get.

The house was aflame. He watched as the firefighters, a good two dozen of them, stood by and watched the flames lick at the house he'd called home for over two decades. They were joking around and holding onto the equipment they had in their hands as if they were drinking beer at a block party.

"You're not even going to try and save it?" The first fireman turned and looked at him while shaking his head. "Don't you think you should make some sort of effort to save even a small portion? I mean, this was someone's home." *Mine!* He wanted to scream at him. The man looked back at the house, then at him. The smile he gave him made Fletcher think of Crane, and he took a step back from him.

"Nah, we did all we could and that was just to keep the other houses on either side of it from going up. But it's a loss…was pretty much by the time the match was lit to start it. By the time we were called in, we knew that there would be nothing we could do. And even if we had the manpower, I doubt whoever owned this is going to come forward." The man looked at the house when the front wall fell into the flames, licking it up as if it were fuel. Which he supposed it was. "There were enough dead bodies in the place when we made our first sweep that we knew that something huge went on inside that place. Scared a few of the younger men, but we got right out and called it in to the cops. The police said they'd straighten it out when it died down. Don't know what they're planning, but there's not going to be much to work with if you ask me." Fletcher had forgotten about the bodies and moved back when told.

His name was not anywhere, so they wouldn't be able to trace this back to him. There were a few things in the house that he might have liked to have collected, but not enough for him to risk going into a flaming house to get. Fletcher knew that starting over again, getting the equipment he needed to play, was going to be time consuming, but he'd just find a better place and make sure this time that he took better care about the bodies. Perhaps he'd set up his own little cleaning service and have them work solely for him. But he knew, just as surely as he was watching his house burn to nothingness, that he'd never do most of the things on the mental list he was forming. He was simply too lazy. He was still trying to figure out where he could go for the time being when he looked around and saw the woman from New Orleans. And she was staring right at him.

She looked different. He supposed it had to do with being Crane's donor, but he had a feeling it was more than that. She looked…well, glowing came to mind, but he knew that wasn't quite right either. As he watched her, he saw Henson and two other woman come up beside her, and then there he was.

"Crane." As much as he hated the man, Fletcher feared him. And when he turned and looked right at him as well, Fletcher lifted his chin and glared. As he watched, Crane took his hand to his mouth and bit down. When he pulled his hand away, he was missing the same two fingers Fletcher was. But his were still attached; Fletcher's were not. Before he moved to tear the man's throat out, someone put their hand on his arm.

"You don't want to do that, I'm thinking. First of all, he'd kill you right out, and what fun would I get to have? Secondly...well, secondly, it would make a nasty assed mess on the ground here, and even though a little sunlight would clean you right out of our lives, there ain't no cause to have all these people seeing you get your ass kicked around the place." He looked at this other man, who hung around Crane all the time, and glared at Rufus. Fletcher had often wondered if they were lovers, but dismissed it when the man laughed. "I'm Rufus, just in case you didn't catch that when you was looking into Sloan there. And I'm telling you that now so's you'll know me when you see me. And I try my best to let the people I kill know my name before I tear out their throats. I'm polite like that. Even to ass whips like you are."

"I think it's ass wipe, you moron. And you think you have it in you to kill me?" Rufus nodded and Fletcher laughed. "I tore you up yesterday and we both know it. Are you slow to heal? Do you need me to find you a wet nurse to bring you back? Throwing you against that wall, did you get a bump on your head from it? You had to if you think you're going to tangle with me and come out on top."

"Nah, I got it covered. I dined on a nice little she-wolf. Tasty little morsel. Then we fucked the night away. What did you do? You kinda smell like...I were gonna say shit, but I think it might have a better scent than you do. I guess not having a thing to change into after sleeping the night away in that there empty building kindsa takes it right outta you, huh?" He looked at his house when Rufus did.

"That's a real shame that you didn't hang around when I set this fucker to light. Did you know that nearly anything we used to light it just went out? I'm assuming you had some sort of curse on the place. I had to think real hard on getting past it. But as you can see, I got it done."

"I did, as a matter of fact. It was supposed to be fool proof, you being the fool. What the fuck did you do?" Rufus laughed again and pointed to his right. There stood the same faerie that he'd hired to cast the spell that would keep him safe. She blew him two kisses as she moved deeper into the crowd. "You must have had something good over her head for her to disobey me. She's going to pay for this. What was it? You have her family?"

"No. Just asked her. 'Course, I did mention how you hurt the alpha and Sloan. And then there was Miss Jade. Did you know that she and that one were on the best of terms? When she found out that you injured one of them there Gem's mates...well, let's just say if'n I was you, I'd better hope I never have to go to ground. I don't think you're going to find it all that comforting. Them faeries, they can be kinda mean when they get their wings all dusted like you done did hers. She and her family are safe, and you'll never get to threaten them again. I promise you." Rufus laughed again when Fletcher shivered. "You done fucked with the wrong family if you're thinking you can simply get away with this. Those Gems, they do know how to protect what they loved more'n anything I done ever did see. And Sloan, he ain't no happier with you than that faerie is. In fact, it's a real toss-up to know who hates you more. 'Course, I'd be real happy if any of them took you out."

Family? He looked back over to where Crane and Henson stood. He could see the woman close to the big vampire and knew that he'd claimed her, but family? Fletcher started to ask Rufus what he meant when he saw Crane put his arm around the woman and kiss her on the head. His woman…Crane had just kissed his plaything.

"She's his mate?" He looked at Rufus when he laughed. "That bitch from Orleans, that's his mate? Did he know it when he stole her from me? I had her first and now…mother fuck, she's his mate? That is so not right. On so many levels."

"I'm thinking he did claim her, but it looks like she don't mind so much. And never seen a more in love couple in my days. I don't want a mate for myself, but seeing the two of them together makes you kinda wish for it to happen sooner rather than later." Rufus cleared his throat. "Oh, and by the way, you might live a bit longer if you don't call her a bitch. She's a might touchy on that. She might be a hell of a she-bitch, but she don't cotton to being called that."

Fletcher started to tell Rufus he could care less what she thought of the term, he was going to call her that when he got her into his lair and started cutting on her, but he didn't. The thoughts of her in his den, her being tied to his walls, made him smile. Fletcher knew that he'd enjoy every scream she voiced and every drop of blood that spilled from her body. But he was standing alone when he started to tell the older vampire. Not just alone, but not where he'd even been standing when the man had walked up to him. Fletcher looked around, trying his best to remember how he'd gotten here and where the hell here was.

Then it occurred to him. He was home. Not the house he'd lived in recently, but the one he'd called home as a child. Was that only just a hundred years ago? Hard to believe. But at twenty-two he'd finally convinced a friend of his to change him to what he was. It had been hellish, but he was something to be proud of, even though his parents had never seen it that way. They'd been more backwards than he'd ever dreamed, stupid in their inability to see what wonderful things could come to them now. His father had been waiting for him, it seemed, when he'd gone back to tell them what he'd done.

"You get on out of here. Don't want your kind hanging around us folks." His father had stood in the doorway to their lean-to house with the borrowed gun in his hands. He knew it was borrowed because his family had had no money and his father would never steal anything. "You heard me. Get yourself on out of here."

"I'm your son, Dad. Let me tell you what's happened to me. There is so many things I can help you with, so many things I can get for you. Let me in, please?" His father had lifted the gun to his shoulder and didn't answer. "At least let me see Mother then. She of all people will understand why I've done this. And I've done this for her especially." It was a lie. He'd done this not with his family in mind but what he'd gain from it. How he was going to live forever. How, and soon too, he was going to have all the things his family had never given him, which was the world.

"She's gone on to meet her maker." It took Fletcher several seconds to realize that his dad hadn't meant that she'd been turned too and was seeing the man who had turned her, but that she'd died. "She done went and died of a broken heart on what you done did. And the shame. She was shamed by what you did. Shamed enough to die at her own hand."

"Let me see her." He knew on some level that he couldn't bring her back, but he wanted to try. "Invite me in and let me see to her. Maybe I can change her too and she can live. I don't want her to die hating me."

"You think I'm gonna let you touch her? With your soiled hands?" His father had laughed. "You always were about as dumb as a rock with a split in it. You thinking...damned if I don't think you do think that. You think she'd be the monster you are? You think...you done broke her heart and now she's gone. And I want you gone too. I'm thinking you done did enough damage to this here family and our name. You're a monster, and monsters don't have families. Get on out of here."

"She's my mother. I have the right to—" The buckshot tore into his skin, and Fletcher knew that if he didn't have someone help him pull it from his body before he fed, he'd be riddled with it. "What the hell is wrong with you? Are you trying to kill me? I'm your son, your only child, and you want me dead? You hate me that much?"

His father's "Yes" had him taking a step back. "I'm not telling you again to get yourself away from here. And don't you be returning either. I've quit of you. I no longer have a son, first born or last. You are dead to me."

Grief took his breath away, and Fletcher moved back into the trees that surrounded his family home. He'd been shunned by the entire town too. And when he'd been able to, he'd left there, never to return. Until now. And he wasn't even sure how he'd gotten here. Looking around, he wondered where the years had gone. It had been fun, up until now. But he was going to overcome this too.

The house, of course, was gone. The one-room shack had been falling down around his parents' head for years before he left, and at some point someone had simply helped it along its way apparently. Now sitting in its place was a trailer. He nearly turned away when the front door opened. He stood mesmerized as people spilled from it, and he felt a sudden connection.

The woman standing there, huge with pregnancy, looked like someone he knew. But he couldn't place her or the man who had come out just ahead of her and helped her down the stairs. As he watched, the young man went back into the house and helped an elderly woman out in much the same way as he had the pregnant one, and helped her sit on the chair with several cushions on it. Fletcher moved closer and pulled the shadows around him to see if he could figure it out.

"I don't think I'm long for this world. I'm just hoping that I can live to see that one being born." The elderly woman put her hand on the protruding belly and laughed a little. "Yep. Who would have thought that I've have me a grandbaby. I wish I had more time."

"You have a great deal of time, Grandma. And we won't hear any differently." Even as far away as he was, Fletcher could hear the older woman's heart skip beats as it worked in her chest. It sounded tired and out of rhythm with the one nearest to him. The young woman continued as she ran her hand over her huge belly. "I'm just sorry Grandda couldn't have lived to hold her. So you have to stick around so you can tell him when you leave us. A long time from now."

The elderly woman looked in his direction. Fletcher didn't move but felt as if the woman could not only see him but could hear his own heart as it pounded in his chest. When she asked for a glass of water, the pregnant woman got up and went into the trailer and the man went with her. Fletcher moved closer and let her see him.

"You're still alive, I see." He nodded, not sure what the hell he was supposed to say to her, but had a feeling that she knew who he was. "I told Momma when she talked about you you'd be too smart to let anyone kill you off. I never heard anyone talk about you in a good way, but I figured if you were her brother, there had to be some good in you."

Fletcher sat down and stared at her. "I don't have any family but.... Do I know you? I mean, you look familiar, but I can't place you. I've not been around for a while."

Her laughter had him remembering again, but it was there and gone too fast for him to catch it. When she settled, he watched her closely as she put her hand over her heart to slow it. Fletcher knew as surely as he was sitting with her now that the woman would be dead before morning. And for some odd reason, that saddened him just a little.

"I'm sure you think you know me, but you don't. My mother...well, you didn't know her either. She was your sister." Fletcher shook his head and the woman nodded. "Yeah. After you left they had another child. My mother. Then after they died, my mother had me. I married late in life; I'm nearly seventy years old, but my heart has always given me—"

"She's dead. She died from a broken heart. My mother, I mean. She was dead and I was her only child. So, whatever you're saying can't be right." The woman laughed again. "Father told me she died. He stood there on our front stoop and told me she'd taken her own life when she found out what I was. He forbade me to come here again because I had killed her."

"He told you that, yeah, but she was living. Her heart was broken and having my mom nearly done her in at that age of her life. Women back then didn't have children at forty, but there my mom was. Not a year after you went and got yourself changed over my mom was born to them.

Grandma never said anything to her, but Mom was saddened by it all. Mom always thought she'd wanted a son, one to replace you. But that didn't happen, now did it?" Fletcher was shaking his head, but she pulled a chain from her neck and showed him a small locket. He felt as if he'd been slapped in the head. "My mother got this when she was married, and I got it when she passed. I'm going to give it to my daughter to pass on to hers. You wanna see the pictures?" She was working at the tiny clasp when he felt as if he was going to be sick. Or pass out. Neither of which he was going to allow.

Fletcher stood up and backed from her. She was lying. His mind screamed at him over and over, *liar, liar, liar*. He moved to the tree line again and stood there as the man and the woman came back out of the little trailer. All he could think of was that this woman was having his great niece. Fletcher watched them and decided that this was another trick Henson and Crane were playing on him. His mother would not try and replace him. He was her only son.

He nearly fell over the mail box as he moved toward the road. But as he sat there in the dirt staring at it, everything in his life, every murder he'd committed, every lie he'd told came rushing back to him. He stared at what had been his parents' mail box. The name was different, of course, but he knew that hand-carved box anywhere. It looked just as his home had looked when he'd gone there the last time. Including the falling down roof.

Fletcher wandered around the town without talking to a single person. Things were not the same, of course. Over a hundred years had passed since he'd been there. There was no way that things could be the same. As he made his way to the cemetery, he had only one thought in his head. His father had lied to him.

The part of the cemetery where his family had been laid to rest was larger than most of the family plots. He opened the little gate and walked in to stand over his father and mother's graves. Staring at the headstone, he thought about how he'd mourned the loss of his mom for decades; still did on occasion. And now he found out she'd not only lived, but had forgotten him altogether. He looked at the headstone.

"Loving wife to Alfred Stone and mother to Shawna Stone. May she find eternal peace in the next world." He laughed bitterly. Her death was ten years almost to the day after he'd been to see them that night. He looked over at his father's grave and spit on the stone there. His father had died a few short weeks after his mom had. Fletcher thought it only fitting. The man could do nothing without involving his *little woman,* as he called her. The grave next to theirs was marked with Shawna Cartwright. She had lived to be only twenty-eight. The stone next to hers said the man had lived to be forty years older before he died as well, only a few months ago. The empty space next to him looked to Fletcher like it was just big enough for the old woman on the front lawn.

No matter how he tried to think of it, Fletcher had been cut from their lives as surely as he'd died that night. And the fact that he was never mentioned in the cemetery, not a marker or even a word on her headstone, made him realize that she'd been hiding from him as surely as his dad had lied. He wanted to go back to the trailer and kill them all for what they'd done to him. Instead, he made his way to the county seat and to the archives to look around.

It was all there. Even his name, his real name of Alfred Stone Junior, had been stricken from the records with a dark mark of a pencil. Beside the name was the word "monster."

Fletcher left to make his way back home. To his home. When he realized he didn't have one any longer, he stood in the middle of a great field and screamed. The birds taking flight, the sounds of the animals scurrying for shelter, didn't make him feel any better. Instead, he made his way to the building that had been his home last night. It was his only safe place.

~~~

"I'd order ten dozen of these. You can always put them back if they don't sell this late in the summer, but I don't think you're going to have that problem." Opal looked at her growing list on the computer. Jade and Diamond had come over early that morning, and then Sapphire and her other two sisters had shown up at lunch time. Opal was so nervous that she was sick to her stomach. It was too much, much too fast.

"What if none of this sells?" All three of her older sisters only snorted at her while Emerald laughed. "I'm in over my head. This will never work as a business. I'll just use the entire space for my studio and that will be fine with me."

"No, it won't. Here. I think you should go with this color tissue paper. It will look really good with the business cards I made for you." Sapphire told her to order six thousand sheets, and Opal just stared at her. "Take a deep breath and change that number from fifty to six thousand."

She did it before she could think not to, and then she stood up. They'd been in her building all day and she suddenly needed to get out. As she moved toward the door, she felt Sloan touch her mind.

*Don't.* He laughed and she tried to think if she could kill him in his sleep when he laughed again. *Do you have any idea how much money this is going to cost me? I'm never going to be able to pay you back. They're spending money like you have billions.*

*I do.* She stopped moving and waited for him to tell her he was kidding. He didn't. *I've been around for thousands of years, Opal. Thousands and thousands. I have a great deal more money than they can spend in several lifetimes. And whatever this costs us, we'll make back in no time. You're going to do fine.*

*What if I don't?* He told her they would. *Sloan, this is insane. I can't run a shop, work on my orders, and not worry about every little penny I spend on this. What if I fail?*

*You won't. But if you think you will then you will. Think of it this way: you have more money than you can spend in decades, you've no overhead, very little expense, and what you do have is all merchandise that will sell. I know it. And if you fail, you just pick up the pieces and try again. You have plenty of time to do whatever you wish.*

She sat down on the chair and thought about what he was saying. *I'm going to live for a long time. A very long time.*

*Yes you will. A very long time. So will your family.* She nodded, knowing that whatever Jade and Quentin had gotten had been spread around to the rest of her sisters. They all would live for a very long time. And their grandmother too. But not Allen. He had told them that he'd just as soon die when his time was up. He had a mate that he wanted to see.

*The order that they're helping me put together...I'm terrified to see the cost.* He told her he wasn't. *What if I do break you? What if I use up all your money and you have to get a job? You can't be out in the daylight. How will we make this all back?*

*The only breaking me I worry about is when you ride me. Do you have any idea how hard I come when you are sitting atop me and taking your own pleasure?* She looked over at her sisters as he continued. *I wish you were here now. Well, not here, but with me now. The meeting I'm in isn't going as I had hoped.* She remembered that he'd been called to a council meeting early this evening, and it was why she'd called her sisters to come and mess around in the shop. A mistake she was less worried about than she was for Sloan.

*They think you should bring him in, alive? They think you should bring that monster in so they can give him a fair trial.* He told her yes. *I think I should hunt this bastard down and tear his throat out. Then piss on him.*

*I like the way you think. Unfortunately, they don't agree with me. Rufus is even getting pissy with them.* She asked him if he'd talked to Blair yet about Ruby. *Yes. And believe it or not, Blair is okay with it. Of course he doesn't know about the sex part, just that she fed him. I don't think he's thrilled about it, but he was there when Rufus was hurt so he knows that he needed to feed. You have no idea how thrilled I was to hear him say that. Christ, it could have gone very badly.*

He laughed, and Opal felt better. *I'm going to try not to worry about this bastard if you promise to be safe. I need your bank account.* He told her he'd try and she stood up. She might as well finish this so she could get back to the house. But before she went no more than a few feet from the door, Rufus was standing in front of her.

"Hey." She still was upset with the vampire but knew that what he'd done to Ruby had been because she'd asked him to. And Opal was having a hard time being even mad, because she knew what it was like to have a vampire make you come. He nodded to her sisters before he spoke again. "I need your help with something. Them girls over there too. I've a plan but I don't know shit about girls and you are the only ones I know."

"And you're needing our help with a woman? Is this poor woman your mate? You're needing our help making your mate like you." He shivered and she laughed, having her answer then. "What do you need the help of girls for? And so you know, none of us are girls. We're all women."

"Yeah, I know'd that. But you can help me. I gots...I have me a problem with one. She's a faerie and she's a mite pissed at me." They moved to the table again and he nodded to her sisters. "I need to make something up to her and she's not having it. Now she's taken liberties with me and...well, I...well she's...damn it all to hell, she's making me crave something I'm not into craving."

"Like what?" He flushed so brightly that Opal laughed. "Sexual in nature? Or has she made you crave the taste of a burger and fries?"

Sloan had been in the kitchen with her last night when Alex was making her some dinner. He'd eyed her sandwich so hard she'd made him take a bite of the sandwich and then a fry. It was all Alex could do to keep up with him. Sloan had eaten seven burgers and four plates of fries before he'd picked her up and carried her to the bedroom to fuck her nearly senseless.

"No, nothing like that. She asked me to do her a favor and I messed it all up." He sat down and she could see that he was really upset. "I never had to pick posies before. Have you ever done it? Well, they all look about the same to me. Weeds with bigger heads than some of the humans that like them. Anyway, she needed this here particular flower and I picked a bunch of what I thought she needed. Turned out...well, I done picked her field of herbs she was growing for something else. Now I don't know how to fix it."

"Herbs. I'm assuming this faerie is someone who has helped you and Sloan in the past." He nodded. "What was she looking for?"

"Purslane. You ever hear of it?" Opal nodded, as did Jade. "I done picked all her chicky weed instead of getting her what she needed. Now she's threatening me with not wanting sex for the rest of my days. And me craving something called a milk shaker. Whoever heard of such a thing?"

"I have some. Purslane, I mean. Not a lot, mind you, but about fifty containers of it. It's not as popular as I thought it would be when I first had it in the store, but now people are picking it up. It's usually thought of as a weed but...." Jade shrugged. "I'll let you have what I have left for cost. I'd have to either plant it somewhere or let it die over. And I might even be able to help you out with the chick weed, not chicky weed."

Rufus nearly took her arm off leading her to the door. He was telling her he'd pay her any price if she helped him out, and Jade was laughing. As they made their way out of the building, Opal turned to the rest of them.

"What do you suppose she needs a field of chick weed for?" No one answered her and she moved back to the table. "I need to see about displays. I've been thinking about going to some estate sales and picking up something like that. Maybe even selling a few antiques too."

"I have some old furniture if you want to use that." She looked up at Sloan and her body reacted to his closeness. His low growl had her smile and he looked at her sisters to continue with what he was saying. "I never throw anything out. It has been...let me just say that I have accumulated a great deal of things over my lifetime. And if you can unload it for me, it might go a long way in recouping some of my loss, since my mate thinks that this is a lost cause." Sloan winked at her and she flushed hotly.

"What sort of furniture?" Opal smiled at her sister. Diamond had a thing for old stuff. Even Emerald perked up at the words "old furniture." "I mean, are we talking about things you made or purchased? Either one will be cool, but I like the crafted stuff better. And how old do you mean?"

"I do not craft. I will leave that to my mate. But really old. And some of it might be rotted by now. It's been a while since I've taken a look at it." He looked at her with such intensity that she stood up. "Would you like to see it?"

Nodding, she locked up her building when her sisters started gathering their things. An adventure was afoot, she thought with a laugh. As they headed toward a long sleek limo, she looked up at him. She was in love with Sloan Crane and she was still shy about it, but it was becoming easier and easier for her to say to herself. Smiling down at her, he helped her into the limo and then slid in beside her. As they rode to the warehouse, she thought of how she was supposed to do this. And when he took her hand in his, everything, all of it, seemed to be okay.

# Chapter 9

*Do you have any idea how much I would like to lay you over this table and feast upon your body? Then take you hard and quickly while you scream out my name?* Sloan had been teasing Opal like this since they'd gotten into the car. He'd expected to find her deep in depression about spending what she considered his money, but she'd been laughing with her sisters. He decided that he'd have to make sure she had some time with them while he rested.

*Behave yourself. I think they know what you're saying to me.* He was pretty sure they did as well and nearly laughed. *What do you think they're thinking right now? That I'm some sort of femme fatal? I'm not, you know.*

*Why on earth would you think that? Good heavens. I left a very important meeting with my council just to come to you and have an evening of unbridled sex. But I find you with several woman having a grand time as if you never thought of me.* She looked so stricken that he pulled her into his arms. *I was teasing you. I'm very happy you and your sisters get together and that they're helping you get your shop ready. It's going to be wonderfully successful. And so are you.*

*You might not think so after you see the bill. I never knew that start-up could be so expensive.* He did but said nothing. It mattered little to him if she spent every penny he had. He'd just like to see her happy. As she moved across the warehouse to see something that Ruby had found, he sat on the large desk that he'd forgotten about. Sapphire came toward him and sat on the corner as well. She was late in her pregnancy and seemed to glow with it. But whatever she had on her mind was making him think he was in deep shit.

"I think she's happy with you." Sloan nodded. "She's blooming. I've never thought of that word to describe someone that was happy, but she is."

"She has made me very happy." He looked over at her. "Are you still upset with me about changing her?"

"No. I know...I saw the pictures." Sloan had figured that the big wolf would share with his mate. "The man that is trying to take her, do you have any leads on him?"

"The house that we burnt to the ground was filled with several bodies. Twenty-three. We took this information to the council and they have said that just because he owns the house, it does not mean that he murdered the people inside." He glanced at Sapphire when she huffed. "I agree. But they don't want anything to come back and bite them in their asses. I don't blame them, but I have made it very clear that if he touches any of you, and I mean *any*, I will tear him apart without thought to seeing if he had harmed you."

Diamond called them over to a large bed. The mattress was there as well, but it was the big bed that had him thinking things better left for their home. When Opal ran her fingers over the carved headboard, he wondered if she'd let him tie her to it while he had his way with her. He could see by the look on her face that she was thinking along the same lines that he was. Making love in the huge bed was going to be something he looked forward to.

"I want this." He nodded, not caring now who was there, and took a step toward her. "I mean at our house. I'd really like to see if you'd mind if we brought this to your house. I'd like to put it into your room if you don't mind."

"Consider it done." She smiled at him and he felt as if the sun were out and he was privy to it. "There are other pieces that match this. A dresser and a few odds and ends. Would you like those as well?"

"Are you going to sell this stuff?" He tore his eyes from Opal, who was blushing, to look at Emerald. "The reason I ask is that if you put this stuff out in the store, she's going to have people asking about it all the time. It would be good to establish up front that you are or not going to sell it. Me? I'd make a killing off this stuff, but I don't think that I could do as good a job as Opal and her store front."

Sloan looked around the warehouse. There were decades of things here, from small kitchen items to larger than this bed pieces of furniture. And all of it was well crafted and well cared for. He moved toward another line of things and saw things he'd not thought of for years, more likely hundreds of years. He ran his hand over an oak table that he remembered taking a few wenches on when he'd first been made. He winked at Emerald, and she grinned. The girl was way smarter about the ways of the world than anyone thought, he was sure.

"It seems a shame to have these things just wasting away here." Emerald nodded. "If I sell them, do you know how to price them? Some of these things are as old as, if not older than, most of the buildings in this part of town."

"Grandmother would know. She loves this sort of thing too." Sloan watched them sort through the rest of the room and he looked at Opal. She was glowing with happiness, and when she threw back her head and laughed at something that her sisters said, he smiled as well.

Suddenly, Rufus was standing in front of him, and Sloan felt the tension almost as soon as he told him there was a problem.

"Fleming is around." Sloan looked around the room, wondering if he meant right there, and was afraid for the family. "I'd say that he's going to have to go to ground soon or he's going to be hurting. That faerie that we knows? Well, her and Ursula, they'd be on the war path for his ass."

"What happened?" Rufus looked at the women, then back at him. "Rufus, what the hell did you do?"

"They helped me out. Not knowing, of course, but they…did you know that purslane can render a vampire sick? Kill him if he takes in enough of it?" Sloan nodded. "I didn't. She…Ursula and Ysane sent me down on some mission of theirs and had me bring them all kinds of that stuff. Didn't tell me that I ought not touch it. I'm glad now that I had me some gloves. But that one there, the Gem that runs that posy shop, she had a shit load of the weed and sold it to me."

As if she knew they were talking about her, Jade turned to them and waved. He had a thought she knew that purslane could kill his kind if enough of it was ingested or handled, and that Rufus had gloves because she'd provided them. Sloan smiled. This family was getting better and better all the time.

"Do you know where he is?" Rufus looked like he might bust. "Christ, what now? Have I told you lately that you're a pain in my ass?"

"That I am. But this here? This is good." He sat down on a Chippendale settee that Sloan thought he'd gotten as a gift from one of his many lovers over the years, and decided it was going to be sold. "That wolf buddy, Henson? Did you know that he and that Fleming feller had a history? I don't mean the kind of history you and that Thad boy have, but one of enemies. They purt'near hate each other. But Henson, he didn't know who he was at first."

"No. I didn't know he had met him." Sloan started to reach for Blair when something occurred to him. "Do you mean Allen, the older Henson, or the son, Blair?"

"Both, actually. The older ran him off his land some time ago. He was poaching off'n his land, it seemed. Not animals mind you, but chasing one of his female pack. He had his sons with him, and when Fleming made some noise about him being this all mightily powerful being or some shit, that boy of his told him he weren't that old. Told him to the month how hold he was."

Sloan looked at Opal, then back at Rufus. He knew that few knew how old he was, how old he really was. He'd not even told his own mate exactly how long he'd been on earth. But to have a being that could pinpoint your age...well, hell. That would be useful in all sorts of situations.

"You do know if he can do that, we're going to have to protect him?" Rufus nodded. "If a vampire finds out that Blair has that ability, one that can tell not just their age, but more than likely their powers too, they'll kill him or capture him for their own use, and none of it will be good. We'll have to talk to him now."

"I done figured that. I invited him here. He thinks you're gonna need him to move some shit for you, but I figured you'd be more apt to get the information from him all casual like than I'd be about it. I won't be as savvy as you." Rufus grinned. "Plus, I got me a bead on Fleming.

Them faeries is working with me now that I showed them how resourceful I can be. And so's you know, Ursula is gonna visit you soon too. She's got a bee in her bonnet that she owes them Gems something."

Sloan nodded. He knew that telling her she didn't was as useful as telling Rufus he needed to update his clothing. The man was still wearing the garb he'd found him in. Sloan was sure it wasn't the same exact outfit, but it was the same swashbuckling style that he'd been wearing the day he'd changed him.

He heard Blair and Allen before he saw them. And both men looked like they wanted to be anywhere but there. Or maybe it was together. They were very tense today.

~~~

Blair looked around the huge warehouse. He had known that someone of money had owned this place, but never figured he'd know him. The building had been built around the turn of the century, and looked as good now as it probably had back then. Even the windows, usually boarded up and broken out by now, were as crystal clear as if he'd had them cleaned daily. When he took Sloan's hand in a shake, he looked at his dad.

"You going to stay?" His father had been tagging after him for two days. He'd asked him several hundred times what was wrong, but all he'd gotten for his effort was the man pissed at him. He had noticed just this morning that he'd been avoiding Annabelle too. It occurred to him then that they'd had a fight. "What did you do to her?"

His dad looked like he wasn't going to answer. But then he looked relieved that he knew. Blair walked around the room, staring at the things without seeing them as his dad spoke.

"I asked her out. She said...I never wanted to go out with a woman since your mom, but I thought we'd have a nice dinner and a few laughs when she didn't have to cook for us all. She 'bout tore me a new butt. What the hell is wrong with a man asking a beautiful woman out?"

"Nothing." Blair had to look away from his dad or laugh. "Just how did the savvy Allen Henson ask her out?"

His dad mumbled something and he turned to ask him to repeat himself. "I said I told her that we could bump pelvis's too if she wanted. I think that made her really mad."

"You think?" His dad flushed. "What the hell is wrong with you? She's...Christ, Dad, she's my in-law. It would be...I don't know, but damn it all to hell and back. You have to fix this."

"I been trying." His dad looked around after shouting and lowered his voice. "I've been trying, but Sapphire hasn't got a thing on stubbornness like her grandmother does. And she told me in no uncertain terms that I'm not welcome there any more either. What the hell do I do now?"

A million and one things popped into his head, but Blair didn't say anything. He looked at Sloan when he walked toward them. The man looked like...he looked like he was afraid of him, and Blair wasn't sure what had happened.

"I have to talk to you." Blair nodded, his wolf shifting along his skin like he wanted to protect him. "I'm not...I don't beat about the bush when I have something to say or ask. And this is one of those times. Can you can tell how old I am?"

"Yes." Blair glanced at his dad, who had stepped in front of him. "I'd never tell anyone. If you wanted anyone to know, I suppose you would have said something."

Sloan nodded and looked around the room. Blair waited, knowing that there was more to his statement than this. When he turned back to him, Blair could see that he really was afraid, and his next words confirmed it.

"You can also tell what my powers are, can't you?" Again Blair nodded. "People would kill you for that, or more likely, they'd take you as a prisoner and make you do things that would...it would kill a lesser man. Do you understand what I'm telling you? They'd more than kill you, Blair. They'd convert you to what they are, regardless of what you are now."

Blair nodded. "They can also try, but I'm not exactly a weakling. I'm also smart enough to know that someone would use me to hurt others. It's why I don't tell anyone what I can do. I've never even told Sapphire or her family. Dad only knows because...well, we've used it before. When he was pack alpha. It saved our lives a great many times."

"Fleming knows." Blair felt his skin crawl. "Maybe not that you can tell powers of every living being in this world, but that you can date him. Having him know that, if he tells someone, then you're as good as dead."

Blair hadn't thought of that. But now that...he had to tell Sloan something else. Something he'd only just discovered when he'd seen him today. It might not go over as well as it might have when he'd discovered it. Then it had made him laugh, but now...well, not so much.

"You're wolf. Did you know that?" Sloan nodded slowly. "Good. I thought...the day we were all hurt you shifted then, didn't you? That's how you were able to get us all out of harm's way that day. I don't suppose you've mentioned it to Opal, have you?"

"No. I wasn't...things have been a little crazy since that day. I have wanted to, but when we're together, I get distracted a little." Blair winced. He didn't want to know what sort of distraction his sister-in-law was to him. Sloan must have realized it and changed the subject. "I'm not sure if it was just a one-time thing. I'm sure that's all it was, and I won't be able to do it again."

Blair shook his head and decided to make him realize that things like this just didn't happen once. He glanced around the room and let his own wolf go just a little. His dad moved back but was still within touching distance of them both if Sloan did something stupid. Nothing happened, but Blair had a feeling that Sloan was just a little too overwhelmed right now to do more than just breathe. But their time was running out if this Fletcher person was coming for him and his family.

"I'm just a vampire. Like I said, it was a one-time thing." Blair shook his head and reached for Sloan's wolf. He stirred along his skin and had Sloan moan. "What the hell was that?"

"I'm an alpha; your alpha, as a matter of fact. I can pull him for you if you want, make you shift, but it'll hurt like a mother fucker. I would suggest that you wait until you're alone or with Opal to do it." Blair backed up a step when he felt Sloan's wolf pull him. "Sloan, you're going to regret this."

He took him. The shift from man to wolf was quick, and Blair would bet painful. As he lay there panting, Blair reached for Opal and had her come to him. She was nearly on top of them before he could tell her what had happened.

"Christ." Blair thought that was a good term. "Who is...Sloan? This is Sloan? What did you do?"

"I didn't do this at all. You did." She looked at him, then back at Sloan, who was growling low in the back of his throat. "I'm thinking that you're a mite too close to us. Back up, but please keep him under control. He's not taking this well."

*I hurt.* Blair nodded at Sloan when he touched his mind. *Will it fucking hurt like this all the time? It certainly didn't when I did this before. Christ, never in all my years have I...how old am I, Blair?*

*It won't hurt if you let it come to you easy. And you're nine thousand eight hundred and fifty-three years old. You were made not in this world, but created in another. Your birth date is January first.* Blair went to his knees in front of his friend. *I would never, not ever, tell a soul what you are. You can trust me on this.*

Sloan looked at him, and Blair stared at him, unflinching. He knew, as surely as he was sitting there, that Sloan could kill him, alpha or not. His vast powers, his unimaginable magic, could end his race with just a thought. Sloan wasn't just a vampire; he was everything.

*I won't harm you.* Blair nodded, relieved. *I will protect you as you have me. Opal...you know that she is what I am as well?*

"Yes." Blair stood up and looked at his sister-in-law. "You're going to have to get him some clothing, and then take him somewhere he can rest. His wolf has hurt him and he needs to heal."

Opal nodded and moved toward Sloan. Blair could feel her wolf as well, along with whatever powers Sloan had given her. He wondered briefly if he should be just a little afraid. Then he looked at the big wolf.

*I owe you my life.* Blair started to tell him he didn't when something moved over him, a calmness that he knew Sloan had given him. *Her name is Ursula and she is Jinn. She will protect you like no one can. And Blair? Please do not touch her unless she invites you to. Her family is more protective than you are when it comes to those she loves.*

The being…a misty being appeared before them all as Opal and Sloan moved back into the darkness of the warehouse. As Ursula seemed to become more solid, he could see her wings and her magic. She bowed before him.

"Do you know what I am?" He nodded. "You will do well not to say my species title until someone allows it, Master Henson. I have been sent to protect you and all that is yours."

"From Fleming?" She shook her head. "Then who? No one but Sloan, and I'm assuming you, knows what I can do. What is there to protect me from?"

"All." She put out her hand while he was still trying to figure out what she meant. "You will allow me to touch what is yours? I swear to you no harm will come from my touch, but only things that you are to need."

"You're going to protect us all?" She nodded but said nothing. "My mate. You'll keep her safe before me?"

"Nah. I will protect you all. It is within my powers to do so. As for Fleming? We have taken care that he will not harm what is now considered ours." He looked at the woman, then his dad. "He will be included as well. Your family is now ours. Once I have touched you, as leader, any and all that come now and after you will be held in the highest regard and protected forever."

The touch of her hand to his nearly had him drop to the floor. There was no pain, none at all, but there was something that felt like a sexual release and a good long nap at the same time. When she smiled, a beautiful veil seemed to have been lifted from her face, and he knew he was seeing the real her. As she faded out, Blair started to stand but stayed where he was just a little while longer, staring at his dad. Standing suddenly didn't seem all that important right at the moment.

"You okay, son?" He nodded, then shook his head. "Yeah, you sort of look like that too. Did she hurt you or give you something?"

"Give." His dad nodded. "About Annabelle. I need you to fix this now, Dad. I can't have you both at odds when there is so much danger about. It's not safe."

"I'll fix it. Today. I swear." His dad looked around the warehouse. "Man has a lot of stuff in here. You thinking what I'm thinking?"

"I hope not. I want to find my mate and make love to her." His dad laughed. "What were you thinking? And if the words 'pelvis' and 'Annabelle' come out of your mouth in the same sentence, I'm going to murder you in your sleep."

"No. I was nervous about asking her out and I might have said the wrong thing. It wasn't good of me to hurt her the way that I did. But I see something here....You think Sloan will give me a break on this stuff? The man is worth more than six of us. And he's not going to ever need the millions he's gonna make off this stuff. I heard him tell them girls to sell it, all but the bedroom set. I'm gonna buy me a nice couple of things for Miss Annabelle. I'm thinking she'd love that fainting couch over there."

"Dad, I'm not so sure a couch is going to get you anywhere." About the time he stood up and started to direct him in another direction, Sapphire came toward him. She was kissing his cheek when his dad pointed the couch out to her and asked her what her grandmother would think of it.

"Oh, Allen. She'll love this. Do you know that Dad had gotten her one right before he died? She sold it when we moved. I think it broke her heart more than anything. I tried to make her keep it, but she had it in her head that we needed the money more than anything. Which we did, but it had meant so much to her." His dad winked at him. "And this will go a long way to you making up for that crude comment you made to her the other day. What the hell were you thinking saying something like that to her? I'm surprised that she didn't take your dick off and make you eat it. I've never...."

As they moved away, he heard his dad telling Sapphire how sorry he was and that he wanted to make it up to her, but his wife wasn't hearing him. She was still berating him as they got into the truck loaded with the couch. Blair laughed all the way back to the house. His father was getting his just desserts and he loved it.

# Chapter 10

"I can let you rent if for a little while. Just until I find someone who can take it for real. I've only just listed it." Fletcher nodded to the real estate agent as he went on and on about rentals and filling them up.

Fletcher knew that the house had been empty for some time. He'd been by it enough times in the last six months to know that people, mostly homeless people, had been using it without paying a red cent. Before he'd called the agency, Fletcher had taken care to have them moved out. The place needed a good cleaning and a few coats of paint. Fletcher figured after that, it would be only slightly above the condemned status.

"I understand." The agent nodded again and smiled. "You said that you'd give me thirty days' notice if you need to have me move out."

He hadn't. He said forty-eight hours, but Fletcher was giving the man enough compulsion that he knew he'd have all the time he wanted no matter what. But the man shook his head.

"No. I told you before, just two days. If I have a renter, I need you out." He tried again, this time nearly zapping his waning strength in the light of the day. "I can't be doing that. If you want to rent this, then that's the way it has to be. Or you can just not rent it at all."

This was the third time that someone had blown him off in as many hours. And the second time he'd tried to get them to do what he wanted by nearly draining himself. Fletcher was starving and tried to tell himself that was it, but he had a feeling it was something, or in this case, someone else that was fucking with him. He knew that the faerie was after his ass too. She'd already taken out his friend, his only friend it seemed.

"I'll take it." The man nodded as Fletcher handed him the cash. That was another thing that he'd been stooped to. He had to find means of getting real money. "And you said that I could move in right away?"

"Yeah. I can have it cleaned up for you this afternoon. Company is new, so if there are any problems, I'd appreciate it if you'd let me know. If they don't work out, I'll be moving to someone else." Fletcher felt his skin tighten, knowing without a doubt who had cleaned his home. "Ever hear of Pristine Cleaning?"

He had. It was the same firm he'd used to get rid of his bodies. When he nodded at the man, he started in on how they'd contacted him just yesterday and offered him a deal of a lifetime. Fletcher wondered if he would be able to get someone else to come in and sweep the place. But that wasn't going to happen. Whatever the company had done to the place—and he was sure that something had been done—he would just have to live with it. He'd used the last of any cash he'd been able to dig up as it was. He looked around the house that had come furnished and shivered.

"Home sweet home." He moved to the stairs. It was the only reason he'd taken the place, because of the space beneath the nasty rooms above ground. The basement was going to serve as his home until he could get everything back the way it was before. And as soon as he had it set up the way he wanted it, Opal Crane was going to be first on his menu.

Going as deep into the darkness as he could go, Fletcher thought about what had happened to him since he'd ended up at his parents' old place. He'd spent a great deal of time, time he could not spare, looking into the records to see if any of the lies the old woman had told him were true. He'd seen the headstones, yes, but those could be faked as well as anything. But what he'd found still depressed him.

The records were true. All of them. Not only were they true, but he could not find a single bit of information that said that he was their son, a man born to them at all. There was no birth certificate, no records of his baptism, nor was he able to find a single thing with his name on it. Until he'd gone to the cemetery again.

Way in the back, about as far as one could get from where his family was laid to rest, was a grave marker. A single stone that only said the name "monster" on it. The dates, his birth date as well as the day he'd come to see them, was all that marred the lovely stone. He'd had to find someone in the offices to help him.

"Yeah, when I first worked here about forty years ago, I asked the same thing of the boss. He told me that it was an empty grave of some family around here. I looked until I thought my eyes were going to fall from my head until I found it. Last name was Stone. Some man by the name of Alfred. They said he'd been some sort of child molester or something. The family put that there, I was told, as a reminder to them not to mention his name ever again. They sure must have hated him. Nary a person come back to put a single flower on the grave either, in all my years here."

Fletcher looked around his new home. It was funny after all these years for him to be calling himself Alfred Stone again. Smiling, he thought about how his father, the lying son of a bitch, must be rolling in his grave about now.

*How you sleeping?* The voice, almost sounding like it was in the dark room with him. Fletcher sat up from the mattress he'd brought down here from the single bed upstairs. He was just reaching for the ball bat he'd brought down with him when whoever it was spoke again. *I'm thinking not so well. Did you have a nice visit with your relatives? I'm talking about the ones above ground now, not the ones you visited at the pretty little cemetery.*

"Who is this?" He looked around harder, seeing things he knew were not there as well as hearing every little tweak the house made. "Show yourself to me. Stop being a coward and come out where I can see you."

The laughter filled his head and that was when he realized who it was. Crane. The motherfucker had somehow found him. But to speak to him…Fletcher started to ask him how he was doing that. But the man spoke before he could.

*You have been very naughty again, haven't you, Fletcher? Or are you going by your birth name, Alfred Stone Junior? Did your parents call you Junior? I bet they did.* A movement to his left had him standing up as Crane continued. *I never met your sister, but her daughter is a hoot. Have you figured out yet that I told her you'd be coming around?* Fletcher wondered then if she was a plant too, but dismissed that altogether. Crane wouldn't have been that cruel. *Yes, I would have. But she really is your niece. A very nice woman too, unlike some of her relatives. And in the event you didn't know, I'm speaking of you.*

"What have I ever done to you? I mean, other than trying to take your mate. She didn't get eaten by me, did she?" He pulled the bat closer to his body and looked around again. "Where are you? Come here and we'll talk this out. Maybe we can strike up a deal."

*Deal? With you? I think not. What am I doing here? And by here, I'm assuming you mean by being in your head. I have to make sure you are caught in the act of killing someone before I can bring you in. And you know as well as I do what they do to people like you when they're brought to justice. It's swift and very final. Do you think they'd let me do the beheading?*

"I'm not going to kill anymore." *Not until you and I meet up*, he thought. "Just come here. You'll see I'm turning over a new leaf. I have a nice house and no equipment in the basement."

*So I can see.* A finger of fear trailed down Fletcher's spine and he pulled himself tighter into the corner. *There is something else you should know. Ursula and Ysane are both looking for you. Ysane claims...and I've no doubt of her statement...that you killed two of her kind. Did you? After being warned not to? Did you kill two of her sisters?*

"It was all Marvin." Crane laughed again, this time making Fletcher think that the man had gone off his rocker. "He has paid the price of killing them, so why should I be bothered by them too? I've not touched any of the faerie since Marvin passed on."

Crane suddenly appeared right in front of him. He knelt down and jerked Fletcher's head back when he tried to get away. The red of his eyes, the white of his fangs shone brightly in the darkness of the room, and made him seem more evil than anything Fletcher could have ever conjured up. When Crane pulled him up, using his throat to do so, Fletcher knew fear like he'd never felt before.

"Marvin was killed by Ursula because Ysane asked her to. Do you know how she kills vampires? You'll wish for the sun, beg for her to remove your head from your shoulders and cry, whimper like a small babe before she lets you die. If she lets you die." Fletcher felt his bladder let go and heard the sound of his urine as it slipped from his body and hit the hard floor beneath him. "You'll do that as well. Piss yourself over and over while she does to you what…nah, worse than what she did to your friend. Ursula will make you suffer in ways that will go down in history. Would you like to know what she did to him?"

"No. I beg of you. No. Just…let me go. Don't tell her you found me. Don't let her know anything of the kind." Crane dropped him and Fletcher fell into his own piss. "You're going to let me live?"

"For now." As Crane disappeared, light blazed in the room for several seconds before it faded out. The heat of it, the brightness of the light, made his skin burn and his body ache. When he was in darkness again, he held the bat to him as he crawled back to his corner. Fletcher Fleming was going to die, and he doubted very much it would be a slow easy death. Crying himself to sleep, he wished that he'd simply met the sun the day after he'd been turned.

~~~

The store was opening in the morning. How she'd gotten talked into this happening now instead of after she finished her orders was beyond her. Opal moved around the room making sure that everything was priced and marked accordingly, and that there was not a speck of dust on anything. She stopped to stare at Sloan when he stood leaning against the wall near her counter.

"You did a fantastic job. And you did it all in just under three days. I'm very proud of you." She nodded and looked around. "I guess you're still mad at me about the orders."

"Overnighting everything was extremely expensive and a waste of money. I told you that we could open in a month and you said you thought now was better. Why did you do it?" He stood up, then moved to the display she and her grandmother had set up. It looked like something straight out of the forties...a modern kitchen for a hard working woman.

"Did I tell you that I had this in my house at one time?" She didn't answer him but watched as he picked up each item...the old fashioned egg beater and then the flour sifter...before putting it back the way she'd had it. "I never used it, but occasionally someone would come along and cook something for the staff. I didn't even know these things were in the warehouse."

He moved to another display, this one from the early fifties, complete with a television set that weighed nearly as much as she did, and surprisingly still worked. He touched the screen, then the chair that sat in front of it. She'd unearthed a set of soft drink bottles to set beside it that she had to really fight with her grandmother to sell. Her grandmother had loved that brand when she'd been younger.

"Why are you here?" He turned to her slowly and she felt her need for him spike. He didn't move toward her but stood watching her as she put her hands on the counter to steady herself. "Sloan, why are you being so nice to me?"

"I'm in love with you." She shook her head and he nodded. "I am. I didn't think it would be possible for me to love, never dreamed of it happening to me. Not after all these years. But here you stand, and I'm so deeply in love with you, all I can think about is that you're mine for the rest of my life."

"There have been others that you probably said you loved as well." He shook his head as he took a step in her direction. "You've never told a woman you loved her? I find that hard to believe."

"Yet it's very true." He was still moving in her direction, a slow, sexy walk that had her mouth dry and her pussy soak at the same time. "I'd like to take you right where you stand. Get down on my knees and pull your panties down from your silken body and drink from you."

She knew that he could smell her arousal, and she opened her legs just a little wider for him. When his nostrils flared, she felt her wolf stir along her body and rumble against her. Sloan touched his mouth to her forehead as he lifted her skirt up her thigh.

"We can be seen in the window." He laughed a little but didn't stop what he was doing. When his finger slid beneath the elastic of her panties, she moaned when he slipped a finger into her wet folds. "Sloan, you're going to make me come."

"That's what I want." He dropped to his knees, then buried his face into her thighs. Opal had to hold onto the counter while he pulled her panties down her legs and then off her feet one at a time. By the time he laid them on the floor beside him, she was ready to scream. "I'm going to eat you."

Opal nodded and watched his face as he leaned into her. She started to close her eyes against the overwhelming feeling he was giving her, but he told her to watch him. Sticking out his tongue, he licked her, opening her nether lips with his tongue and sliding it over her clit. Opal cried out when he began to worry the small nubbin with his tongue.

"Come for me." Her body imploded as it did what he commanded. Twice more he ordered her to come, to have her fall apart then be put back together. Opal's legs were no longer strong enough to hold her when he stood up. Lifting her up, he sat her naked bottom on the counter and stepped between her legs. "I'm going to fuck you now. And when you come this time, I want you to bite me hard. Mark me."

"Yes." He tore his pants open and she reached for his thick cock. Wrapping her fingers around him, she watched as he moved to and fro as if he were already deep inside of her. When he put his hand over hers, she looked up at him. "I'd like to taste you this way."

She moved off the counter and onto the floor in front of him. Taking him into her mouth, she moaned at her first taste and nearly cried out when he began moving in and out of her mouth as he had her pussy so many times since she'd met him. Opal felt him touch the back of her throat twice before she swallowed him down past the tight muscles, and was rewarded with his low growl.

"Again. Do it again." She loved the taste of him, the way his salty cum filled her mouth each time he moved in and out of her. When she cupped his hot balls in her hand, she nearly cried out again when he tore her from his cock and stood her up. "Turn around. I have a need to fuck you like a wolf."

Her own wolf snarled at her. She did as he told her, but her wolf wasn't happy about it. As soon as he entered her, he took her hard from behind, his big hand wrapping around her hip. His other dug into her pussy and tugged hard at her clit just as he sank his teeth into her shoulder. Opal screamed out her release, then came a half dozen more times as he fucked her with his cock and fingers. She was ready to beg him to stop when he came deep within her.

Her body, exhausted from what he'd given her, seemed to renew its energy when he pulled from her quickly and stepped back. His wolf took him so fast that she had only a second to realize that her wolf was coming too. She let her wolf slide over her in much the same way he'd moved in and out of her only moments before.

He growled at her when she tried to move away. But his wolf was scaring hers and he must have realized it. When his wolf reached for her this time, she moved closer to him, but not in a position where he could take her. Instead of ordering her to do as he wanted, he held her under his massive paw until she calmed.

*I'm sorry.* She looked up at his chocolate eyes and could see that he was very sorry. *I seem to have no control over this beast yet.*

She snuggled her wolf up to his and he held her. Her body, her wolf, wanted him now, and she was nearly purring to him to take her. As he mounted her, gently this time, she laid her head to the floor and gave herself to him. As soon as he entered her, filling her with his cock, she came, howling loudly as he took her hard and fast. As soon as he sank his canines deep into her shoulder, she came again, this time letting the darkness take her. The last thing she heard was him howling out his release as he filled her again and again. Opal was well and truly his mate.

# Chapter 11

Annabelle tried her best not to be excited about the pretty chair. But she was still just a little angry with Allen. He'd...he was crude to her. Not that she hadn't given some thought to sex, but not with him. Not with her grandson-in-law's father. It was just too —

"Well?" She looked at Ruby as she sat at the kitchen table. "Have you sat in it or not? I think it's perfect for you. All this melodrama that's been going on with you and him. So? He wanted to take you out, then maybe have sex...is that so bad?"

"I'm old enough to be his mother." Of course she should have known that Ruby wouldn't understand. Her snort made Annabelle want to smack her in the head. "I'll have you know that I'm very picky about who I have sex with."

"I'm sure you are. But a simple no would have been better than what you did to him." Ruby sipped her tea before continuing. "Don't you think that shifting and chasing him around the yard, then peeing on his car...and whatever else you did to him...was just a little over the top?"

"I was upset." She'd been embarrassed. "He thought it was funny until I told him never to come back here. I suppose free room and board is a way to his heart."

"Is that what you think?" Annabelle didn't answer. In truth, it wasn't, but she was hurt too. "He does more around here than anyone. Last week, before you threw him off the property, he fixed my car, hoed three rows of potatoes for you while you were at the doctors, washed up the dishes that wouldn't fit in the dishwasher, and did a load of laundry and hung it out. I'd think he'd be better off if he took money from us than room and board."

Annabelle got up and started to fry up some bacon. It hurt her more than anything that she didn't know how to take back some of the things she'd said and done to her friend. He'd been crude to her, yes, but he'd been joking. Surely a man such as him wouldn't want to have sex with an old woman like her. Who would, to be honest? She looked at Sapphire when she came into the kitchen. Her eyes were bright and her face pale.

"How long?" They both looked at Ruby. "How long have you been in labor, and how far apart are the contractions?"

"I can't be in labor today. I have two meetings with potential clients and I have—" Her scream nearly made Annabelle faint. The girl was going to die, she just knew it. "Ruby, get Blair. I think he needs to help me."

"I'm here." Blair picked his wife up by scooping her into his arms. Then he kissed her. "I told you when you got up that you were in labor and to stay put. What am I going to do with you?"

As he turned with Sapphire in his arms, Ruby grabbed Annabelle's arm before she could follow. "Are you going to call Allen? It wouldn't be right for him to miss this, don't you think?"

Annabelle nodded. "I hurt him more than he hurt me. I shouldn't have...I just was embarrassed and hurt. I didn't...I don't know how to fix it."

Ruby kissed her on the cheek before she answered. "Share this with him. Call him up, tell him you've been a horny fool, and tell him you have a vibrator."

Annabelle was still standing there when she heard Ruby laughing down the hall. *Impertinent brat*, she thought. Going to the phone to call Allen, she thought of the million ways she was going to get back at her. There was just too much talk about sex in this house, and she needed to put her foot down.

He answered on the first ring.

"Sapphire is in labor." He didn't say anything and she closed her eyes against the tears. "I'm an old fool. A very old fool and I've hurt you. Will you come and be with your family and forgive me?"

"I don't...forgive you for me being an idiot? I don't think so. I was the fool and...well, hell woman, I've missed you. And the girls, but you...we're friends and I shouldn't have...I just shouldn't have." Annabelle cried harder, and she heard him talking to her.

"I've missed you too. Very much. I can't even go out to the...I love my chair. It's in my room and I look at it all the time." She heard him sigh and laugh a little. "And the color is so beautiful. Sloan said you picked it out for me right away. I was going to tell you that you spent too much, but I can't seem to part with it."

"I wanted you to have it. It suits you. I can see you laying there with that reading thing you call your treasure and reading them bodice rippers you like." He laughed a little. "Listen to me. I sound like a love sick old man. And Annabelle, I do love you. Not like a mate but…well, I love you very much."

Her tears burned her cheeks as they fell. She tried twice to speak, to tell him what she felt, but in the end, sobbed out her love for him as well. They were sobbing like children when Opal and Sloan walked in the door.

Sloan stayed back, but Opal held her. As Sloan took the phone from her, she could hear him talking to Allen, but her granddaughter was leading her to the large staircase, and then to Sapphire's room. They were all there by then, except for Allen, who Sloan said was on his way. It was time. The baby…her great-grandbaby…was about to be there.

After shooing everyone out except for her, Diamond, and Ruby, the room was prepared. For weeks now they'd all been taking things from the room so that everything would be ready and putting things in that would be needed in the event that things went wrong. An hour and a half later everything was set up, and Sapphire was dressed in Blair's shirt and nothing else. She looked like a queen, albeit a sweating one, but looked as regal as she did every day.

"How you feeling?" Blair moved into the room and kissed Sapphire. "I wanted to tell you Dad is here. He said that if you have a girl, he'll be as happy as a clam. I told him we didn't care so long as it's healthy."

"You want a son. Admit it." He flushed and nodded. "All these women in this house? I'm betting you want someone here that might understand you a little better."

"I have other men here, but to have a son or daughter…really, honey, you just be healthy for me." Sapphire nodded just as another pain took her. Blair held her hand and Annabelle held her breath. Things were moving right along now.

"All righty now. We're going to check you out, and if you're near to giving this kid his birthday, then we'll get this show on the road." Ruby winked at her before she spoke again. "I've never delivered a baby before. Do you think it's all that hard?"

Sapphire paled and everyone laughed. They knew that Ruby had delivered a few babies since she'd been a doctor, and a few even before that. Diamond too for that matter. As the exam was finished, Ruby told them it was time, and when the next contraction started to build, she told Sapphire to push.

The baby was being stubborn. After an hour of pushing, Sapphire was exhausted and upset. Blair was running out of things to say to her to keep her focused, and Annabelle could see the worry on her other granddaughters' faces. Stepping up to the bed, she pulled Sapphire's face to hers and told her to look at her.

"You want this child in your arms?" She nodded but closed her eyes. "Listen to me, young lady. I did not raise you to be a quitter. Straighten up and push this baby out. I have a meal to cook, and you playing around at this labor thing is making me get a late start."

The next time she felt a contraction coming on, Sapphire glared at her and pushed hard. Annabelle wondered if the baby would be projected across the room, but before she could tell her to calm down, there was a soft mewling sound and then a lusty cry. Her grandson was here.

He was perfect. Ruby handed her to Blair first, and he held him like he was holding the most precious thing in the world. She supposed he was, and the man looked like he did when he looked at Sapphire, full of love, already. When Sapphire took him, Blair watched the two of them so intently that Annabelle felt her wolf stir. The need to protect this little family was making her wolf want to come out and bar the door. Instead, she calmed her by telling her about the baby.

His head was covered in the darkest downy hair. His nose, rounded and small, looked like Sapphire's when she'd been a babe. Long, strong fingers that wrapped around his father's finger looked capable of stretching out and picking up balls. She looked into his eyes when he turned to her, and he had the eyes of a man as old as her.

"He's beautiful." Annabelle nodded at Sapphire. "Would you like to hold him before everyone else comes in?"

"Oh yes." Taking him into her arms, she looked down at his face and felt the tears burn again. Here was what life was about...the next family to carry on. "Your parents would have been so proud today. Just look at him. Your father would have been howling at the moon over him. And your mom? My goodness, she would have just about had a fit over this."

"I think they can see him." Annabelle nodded and touched the soft cheek. "We've named him. But...well, we want everyone here when we announce it."

"Well of course you do." Handing the little man back to his mother, Annabelle kissed both Blair and Sapphire before moving to the door. "I'll bring them in, shall I?"

At their nod, she opened the door and nearly fell back at the amount of people in the hall. It looked like the entire pack was there, and some more spilled down the long staircase. A hush went over the crowd as she cleared her throat.

"It's a boy." The cheer that went up made her heart sing with joy. "Both are doing great. He's lovely, just lovely. And Sapphire has never looked better. Blair, of course, is as happy as they come."

Her other granddaughters moved up beside her, as well as Sloan and Allen. Her grandsons, both Thad and Quentin, were there as well. Even little Angie was begging to see the little man. Rufus stood back, but she moved him up with them. The man was as much a part of the family now as the rest, and she took them all in to meet the newest pack member. While she'd been gone, the bed had been made, the room cleaned of anything to do with the birth, and the baby was dressed in a little shirt and diaper. Even her old rocking chair had been pulled from the corner.

Allen sat in the chair and was handed the baby. He looked good sitting there holding him, and she was glad that she'd remembered her cell phone. Snapping pictures, she was told to sit so she could have hers taken as well with the little man, and smiled at the camera when Blair told her to. This was a day she knew she'd never forget. But she also knew that they, Blair and Sapphire, had to have some time alone, and started to gather her brood up.

"Wait. We wanted you guys to be the first to know his name." Blair held his little boy up for them all to see. "Meet Carter Allen Blair Henson. My son."

"Oh my." Carter had been her maiden name, and Annabelle was so proud that she burst into tears. As she was being held by Sloan and Allen, she just sobbed and sobbed. Finally she looked at Blair. "You've no idea...none at all...what you've done for his old woman."

"When we meet this old woman, we'll tell her you're trying to move into her territory." Blair kissed her on the cheek. "You're happy then?"

"Yes. More than...I've never been so happy." Hugging him to her, she left the room. The rest could leave or not, but she needed a minute.

~~~

Allen followed her out. He really did love this woman, and he wanted to be with her more than he ever thought he would after his own mate had passed. He found her in the kitchen fussing over a pot roast and wiping at her tears. He stood behind her while she blew her nose and then washed her hands.

"He's a sparker, isn't he?" She nodded and turned to him. His heart hurt to see her eyes swollen and red, but her smile made his own come forth. "You're not going to cry anymore, are you? Kinda pulls at a man's heart when a beautiful woman cries."

"No. What a thing to say." She turned from him and he watched as she wiped her cheeks again. "I was wondering...would you help me pick some green beans for dinner? They're about all gone this late in the season, but there will be enough for dinner."

They were both out in the afternoon sun within minutes. He was bent over pulling the plant from the ground when he felt a small tremor of something come over him. He stood up and looked to the woods behind him just as Annabelle did the same.

"Trouble?" He nodded at her. "Do you think it's that Fleming person? It would be just like him to ruin a perfect day."

"He won't." Allen watched the tree line until he spotted something, but he knew as surely as he was standing there that it wasn't Fleming. "Do you see that? Do you know that person?"

"No. I've never seen him...no, that's a female. A woman. I've never seen her before." They continued to watch as the person made her way toward them. The closer she got the better he could make her out. He still didn't know her, but he did reach for his son to tell him someone was there.

"Hello." The woman was...well hell, she was simply magic. And her eyes looked so blue, so crystal-like blue that they hurt to stare at them. When she laughed, he decided that she was carrying bells to go along with the most beautiful laugh he'd ever heard. "My name is Ursula. I'm a friend of your family."

"The faerie." She smiled at him but didn't answer. "You're not a faerie, though, are you? You're...I don't know what you are, but you're not a faerie."

"She's not." Sloan walked up beside him and Annabelle and bowed before the woman. "She's Jinn. She's...she's here to see me."

"And the child. I have a gift for him." Allen watched her as she seemed to float toward Annabelle. "You are very good, are you not? I have a gift for you as well. May I share it with you?"

Before Sloan's warning of "Don't," Annabelle took her hand. When she dropped to the ground, Allen's first instinct was to shift and tear the Jinn apart. But Sloan held him back at the last second.

"She's not hurt her. She never would." Allen started to ask him why he'd told Annabelle not to touch her when he continued. "I thought she should explain first what she was imparting. I didn't want Annabelle to get something she wasn't aware of."

"She is too good not to have it. I don't share often, Master Sloan, and this you know." He nodded and Allen was freed. "I have a gift for you as well. It will…I believe it will serve you well in the coming days."

He took her hand. The power that surged over him made him slightly ill, and he, too, dropped to the ground. As he sat there he looked at the woman who had done this to him, and she smiled.

"What was that?" She smiled again and bowed before him. As she made her way to the house and inside, he looked at Sloan. "What the hell did she just do to us?"

"She gave you…well, hell, she gave you everything." Sloan went inside the house before Allen could decipher what he'd just said. He looked over at Annabelle, who was standing again.

"I feel…goodness, Allen, I feel amazing." She did a little jig in the dirt and laughed like a school girl. "This is…I feel twenty again. I could…would you like to go dancing? I want to go dancing. Tonight after dinner, let's go and tear up some floorboards."

He agreed to go and was hauled up from the ground so quickly that he nearly fell again, and now that he was standing, he, too, felt younger. Vibrant and even a little mischievous. Allen hadn't felt this good in a decade or two. Finishing up the green beans with new vigor, he noticed he was whistling. And Allen hadn't done that in years. After they were done with the beans, they had so much energy that they hoed up the ground for a few potatoes, as well as some squash that had been missed.

In short order they had stripped the last of the vegetables from the garden, cleaned up the dead or dying plants, and put them into the compost pile. They had cleaned up the garden for next season in about a third of the time he thought it should have taken. He moved into the house to help snap the beans while Annabelle cut up some tomatoes to put in a brine to soak. He grinned when he thought of telling Blair he was going dancing. Allen looked at the doorway when Opal was suddenly there.

"What's happened?" She only stared at him until Sloan came up behind her. When he sat her in a seat and asked for some water, Allen looked at the big man, who looked completely lost. He asked again what had happened.

"Her assistant just called her."

The store; he'd forgotten about the store opening today and figured it was about closing time for it.

"She called to tell Opal about her day and how things had gone. And she wanted to make sure that Opal was aware of it so she wouldn't be surprised when she got there later."

"That was nice of her, right?" Sloan nodded and smiled. He had no idea, but that sort of smile coming from a vampire didn't really make Allen feel good. "Whatever the sales were, honey, I'm sure you're going to do much better tomorrow. And if not, then...well, people have to find you and all. We have to expect that a learning curve with this sort of—"

She was shaking her head at him and Allen sat down. He didn't want her to give up so soon. Opal needed this as much as he did gardening. Before he could tell her that, she finally spoke.

"I made just over thirty thousand dollars today." He looked at Sloan, who nodded at him. "We sold almost all the furniture, and nearly every piece of my jewelry and my crafts. There was a run on the soaps that I had gotten at the last minute. They were buying them as quickly as she could unpack them. Some of them didn't even get priced, they wanted them so badly. They're...she sold all of it. I'm...I'm.... What am I going to do?"

"Get busy?" She laughed a little and he smiled. "I'd say that's not too bad for a first day. I'm thinking…hell, you might need to get you another building just to hold you some extra stock."

"Oh no. It was just a fluke. People just came in and…and they felt sorry for me." Allen snorted. "Well, they might have."

"Honey, people don't spend thirty grand because they feel sorry for somebody. They spend that when they love the shit out of the stuff you have for sale. I'm guessing we're making another trip to that warehouse of yours, too. I might even be persuaded to help move stuff this time."

As the couple left to go to the store, Allen finished up the beans. This was turning out to be one hell of a day, and he thought maybe that things could only get better tomorrow.

# Chapter 12

The die was set. He was going to go out with a bang and take as many people as he could with him. Fletcher was sick to death of hiding in doorways, starving for fear of being seen, and most importantly, he was fucking tired of looking around corners for Crane or Henson to come after him. He was infinitely more powerful than either man, and it was about time they realized it.

"I may be just a simple vampire, but I'm a bastard of one. And they will not continue to win over me." He moved along the dark alleys until he was standing in front of the little store that had just opened. He peeked in the big window and wondered if he could go in there to rest for the night. But movement had him moving around the corner into the next alleyway. He saw them before they saw him.

The woman...his woman...was dressed like she'd been out on the town; short skirt, silky blouse, and heels that made him want to watch her walk away from him just to see if her calves would look as good as he thought. The thought of dining on her legs had him stepping out into the light before he could think it was a bad idea. And once there, he leapt at her.

Tearing her from the arms of Crane had him laughing. Using her as a shield, he held her body to his even as Crane reached for her to no doubt pull her from him. As far as Fletcher could see, he had the upper hand in this. But it was the smile on the other vampire's face that gave him pause, and if he was honest, a little fear.

"You want her?" Crane only leaned against the building and stared at him, not answering. "Fuck you, you can't have her. She should have been mine back in New Orleans, but you took her from me again in Paris. Very badly done of you. And you know what I like to do to my pretty ladies once I get them."

"I don't think you have the means or the balls to touch her beyond what you are right now." Fletcher licked her throat and was surprised when she did nothing but let him. Maybe she'd missed him; maybe she needed someone else fucking her. He said as much to Crane.

"Miss you?" The woman in his arms laughed. "I don't think so. But I was always taught to be gentle with the insane. You never know what might set them off. Do you have a list handy that I can use, maybe? Like what would be at the top of your list, if you—"

"I'm not insane." He had to take several breaths to calm himself. He certainly sounded that way, even to himself. "I'm not insane. I'm just a man who happens to like his meals with company. You should be pleased that I've picked you to be my greatest creation. I might just cut you up very little at a time until you satisfy my every need."

It was something Marvin said to him before. "A man who eats alone is boring. A man who eats while the people he carved from watches is someone I admire."

"As I said before, I don't think so." She didn't struggle with him or even try to get away. He knew she had her reasons, but it was Crane that had him nervous. The man looked as if he had not a care in the world.

"Don't you care that I've just marked your mate? Doesn't it bother you at all that I'm going to take her to my lair and carve her up for my dinner?" Fletcher laughed. "You must really hate her to just stand there."

"Nope." That was all he said and it infuriated Fletcher to no end. But the next time he spoke, Fletcher felt his body tense up. "I'm just waiting on back up. I, too, have heard that you never get a crazy person all riled up when you're alone with them. As she said, you never know what the hell they're going to do. Besides, if you think she's going to let you take her, you're not just insane, but stupid as well."

Fletcher wasn't sure what to do. He wanted to run...toss her to Crane and run until he was as far from there as he could go. But he wanted this woman more than he needed to breathe. She'd been the cause of everything that had gone to shit in his life. Before he could make the decision about what to do, Sloan straightened up and bowed.

He felt her before he saw her. Ursula had always been one he'd been afraid of more than the sun. She could and would do things that would make even the strongest of men whimper. And the fact that she'd been looking for him since she'd killed Marvin...well, he was scared shitless. The description was something he'd heard said before and thought it perfect. He watched her as she stood in front of him and smiled.

"You have learned very little in your years as a vampire, haven't you?" He didn't answer her, sure it was a trap. "No matter how many times I have given you a walk, you still seem to meddle with things that do not concern you."

"She's mine." Ursula shook her head and smiled at him, not a friendly smile but one that had the hair on the back of his neck dance. "I found her first. She was in my arms when he took her from me."

"But she was not yours to keep, and even then you knew it. She was never meant to be yours. And now that you have taken her again, there is no choice for me but to intercede." He didn't understand her and he looked at Crane. "Master Sloan will no longer have to follow the rules of the council concerning you. I have taken over for them."

"You're going to let him kill me? Over a woman?" Ursula only shrugged. "That's not very fair or sporting of you. I found her first. That should count for something."

"It might have at one time. Very much so in your favor had you given up on her when he told you she belonged to him." Ursula stepped back and Fletcher had a sudden fear that she was going to kill him. And he wanted to die quickly, not by her hand.

She touched his arm as she moved by him, and he felt the pain of it all the way to his toes. Screaming, he let go of the woman and grabbed his body. Everything hurt; everything seemed to be on fire, too. As he dropped to his knees, she stood over him and Fletcher looked at Sloan.

"Kill me. Please? Don't let her kill me like this." Crane laughed and held onto his mate. Even in all this agony, all this fire that ran through his veins, he could see his love for the woman. "I want to die quickly."

It was her laughter that had him crying. Ursula was going to make him suffer in ways that he'd never dreamed of; make what he did to his victims look like child's play, and what he'd done to others seem like nothing in comparison.

They were transported to a room where he could see, but could not make out what it was. Pain...he was insane with it. There were people everywhere, some of them dressed as his tormentor was, others in clothing like he was wearing. When one of them picked him up and tossed him onto a table, he screamed in pain. Whatever it was that he was laying on was cutting deep into his body.

"It is silver." Fletcher tried to pull from it but only made matters worse. It dug into his flesh no matter what he did. When the man who had put him there shoved him down harder onto the spikes of pain, Fletcher screamed and passed out.

He woke in pain...not just pain, but something he would liken to murderous pain. As he looked around, he noticed that while the room was clearer, the things in it were not. There was equipment here that he'd never seen before. And when he looked harder at one such piece, he felt his body freeze in terror.

"Do you not like what we have done with him? Marvin was bad...not nearly as bad as you, but he was warned not to kill one of us again. Drinking from the faerie was fine to a point, but we did warn you both not to kill."

He nodded, still staring at the body, or what was left of the body of what once had been a man. When Marvin lifted his head and looked at him, Fletcher screamed again. He was still alive. What they'd done to him, what they'd cut from him, they were keeping him alive to continue.

His body had been ravaged. Not by someone cutting it away, but teeth...fangs too, he was sure, as well as the maggots that crawled all around some of the more putrid parts of his body. Large bites had been taken from his thigh and his belly, and one arm was missing. Blood dripped into a bowl beneath him as he stared at him. Fletcher tried to think why he wasn't screaming when he opened his mouth. Nothing was there...no teeth, no tongue, not even gums were left in the vacant spot. He looked at Ursula.

"Please kill me." She nodded and he felt relief for all of a second. "Now, kill me now. Please, I beg of you, kill me now."

"I'm afraid that just won't do, Alfred Stone, Junior. There are many crimes you must pay for, and it must begin now." The sound of a saw starting had him looking at the man standing at his head. "He will start to cut you away now. And so you know, we will continue this for so long as you have lived, all of the years in which you made others suffer at your hands. Then, just because we can, we will add more years to your sentence for the pain and suffering you caused your beloved family. I think I will enjoy this more than any other. My friend was among your last victims."

As soon as the saw touched his skin, he screamed. They were cutting at his jaw when everything went black. Fletcher hoped that he'd never live through this, and began to pray that he wouldn't. But he had a feeling that he would, and when they were finished with him, he'd welcome death with opened arms.

~~~

Sloan paced. He didn't even know where to begin, he was so upset. And every time he looked at Blair, the man had the nerve to laugh at him. He wondered if he knew just how close he was to being killed.

"You do know that she's a lot stronger than she looks, right?" Sloan didn't know what that had to do with anything, but listened as Blair continued. "And the fact that she is paying you back, plus a percentage of what she made off the antiques, is only good business sense."

"I don't want her money." He snapped his mouth closed when he realized how Neanderthal he sounded. That, of course, only made Blair laugh harder. "What if your wife tried to pay you back for the building you gave her?"

"She did." Sloan stopped pacing and looked at the large alpha. "With interest, too. And so you know, I was a little pissy about it as well. But in the end it was a sound decision on her part."

"She paid you back with...oh I see, you mean giving you a son?" Blair shook his head. "Are you telling me you actually took your wife's hard-earned money? And smiled about it?"

"I did say I was sort of pissy, didn't I?" Sloan sat down and rubbed his hand over his face as Blair continued. "What really has gotten you all hot and bothered? The fact that she no longer needs your money, or the fact that she's doing so well? Or is there something I'm not seeing that you can enlighten me on?"

"First of all, I really hate you right now. I want her to succeed." He did too, and could see on Blair's face that he believed him. "What I don't want is for her to feel she owes me for any of it. I wanted her happy. This does not make me happy."

"You wanted her to be happy, or you? Sounds like sour grapes to me." He had no idea what that meant, but got up to pace again. "Did you think she'd do this well?"

"Yes," he answered without hesitation. "I knew it would do this well from the start. She had a good head on her shoulders once she decided that she had to use it...or I guess found the confidence to use it. I know that sounds bad, but she nearly had to be shoved into this. And now that she is doing it, she's giving it her all."

"So that's it." Sloan turned to look at Blair when he didn't continue. "You want her to succeed, but at your pace, and you hate that she's doing so well...so well that she no longer needs you."

"I didn't say that." But it rang true. When he'd gone to the warehouse with her early that morning, she'd already marked what she wanted and what would have to wait...things he'd wanted to do for her, to advise her on. "She knows what she's doing. And doesn't need me."

"I doubt that's true, but I know how you feel." Sloan was hopeful for a second. Then Blair laughed. "I said I know how you feel, not that I agree with you. You hate the fact that she can make this work, when you feel the need to not just protect her, but provide for her and keep her close. Does that sound about right?"

"That's it." Blair nodded. "What the hell am I supposed to do now? She's making this business...did you know that she's had people email her about some of the things that were posted on her website? I've no idea how that really works for her, but she is making arrangements for things to be shipped all over the country. And these idiots are paying extremely high prices for it to be theirs. And her things? She's brought in more staff, seven now, to do what she needs. I have no time with her."

He realized then that was the real problem, and Blair only stared at him without comment this time. Sloan missed her. Not just being with her, but having her at his side. Her laughter and her smile. He started to pace again, this time with purpose. He was going to bring her back to him.

"Want a suggestion?" Did he? More than likely not. This man was related to her through his own wife. Would he give him anything that would make it worse? He didn't think so and told him yes. "Marry her."

"Marry her? I don't understand. Marry her for what reason? We are mates; she is mine and I'm hers." Blair nodded. "You mean perform the ritual that humans do? Actually go to a man of the cloth and say words that mean less to me than...than those things she sells?"

"It will mean something to her." Sloan started to tell him he was insane, but thought about how she had talked for hours about her sister's happiness with her husband. Not mate, but husband. He remembered the look on her face, too, when Blair had presented his wife with a diamond ring after their child had been born. She'd been...she'd been so happy for her.

"I know nothing of romance." Which was true. He'd never had to woo a woman, only to look into her eyes and give her what she wanted as he took what he wanted. "I've been around longer than anyone, and I have no idea how to make one woman as happy as I can."

"It just so happens that I know just the man for you. Well, men. You've met your brothers-in-law, right? They can get you started on the right track and get you moving." Sloan nodded, almost afraid to admit he was terrified. "If I were you, I'd avoid my dad. He knows women, but his style is a little on the...the 'get you arrested' side."

"I heard that." They both looked at the doorway where Allen was standing. "I'll have you know that I have had my dance card filled before many a man in my younger days. And I'm not doing too badly right now, either."

"I don't wish to simply dance with my mate, Allen, but to make her happy." When Allen wrapped his arm around his shoulder, all Sloan could think of was he was in deep shit. He looked at Blair to get some help, but the man was laughing too hard to pay attention. Sloan just knew he was going to regret this, and followed the man out of the house and to the car that was waiting for him.

The trip to town was made mostly with Allen talking about things he'd done for his lady friends, as he called them. While he talked and talked, Sloan reached for Opal and could feel her frustrations. He almost smiled when she told him that she was going to kill the next person who asked her if she'd robbed a bank.

*What is wrong with people?* He didn't answer her because he'd been wondering the same thing for decades. *I mean, where do people get off asking such a question? I hung up on one man. He had the nerve to ask me if I wanted to come with the bed he bought. Moron.*

*What's his name?* His own beast along with his new wolf wanted blood. But her laughter had him settle back down. *Opal, have I told you lately that I love you? And that more than anything in this world, I want to keep you safe and with me?*

*I love you as well.* He felt her send love to him, and he felt wrapped up in it. When she told him she had to go, he felt as if he'd been given a great gift of her love. He looked over at Allen, who was smiling at him.

"I need to buy her a ring. An opal. With diamonds." Allen nodded. "And I need to make a stop first. You can't go with me, but…I need to make a stop."

"Sure. Sure. Just tell me where and we'll go there first." Allen laughed again. "You look like a man that has been told he could have anything he wanted for Christmas."

Sloan shook his head. "I'm a man that has been given every present he's ever wanted, and then some. I'm a man in love with his mate."

"Good for you." When they stopped, Allen stayed in the car. Sloan made his way into the small yet well-kept building that meant little to anyone but himself, and occasionally Rufus. It was the first doorway into many, and one wrong door would get you killed.

Sloan made his way through the maze of doors that would lead him to his home. Not the one he had here on earth, but the one that had given birth to him and his kind. When he asked and was granted permission to enter the large chamber where the king and queen were located, he bowed low before them and waited. He knew this would piss them off.

"Get up. Why are you forever pissing me off?" He grinned but stayed where he was, loving that his father fell for this every time he came to see him. "I swear to you, he is entirely your son. There is no way that I sired such a pain in the ass as this one is."

"You love him." Sloan winked at his mother. "Get up here and give me a kiss. I've miss…what have you done?"

Her voice sounded surprised but not mad. It was what he'd hoped for. "I've found my mate. And she's a wolf. At some point, she changed me to what she is. She is a vampire too. You'll love her as much as I do."

"Good heavens. Where is she?" His dad stood up and ordered the gates to be opened. "We'll have you here. You'll stay in…no, that won't work. We'll have to rebuild that part of the castle. Damned vermin came in and ate away all the wall hangings, and your mother decided that—"

"Dad?" He stopped blustering and looked at him. "I'm in love with her. I'd like to bring her here and marry her. That is, if you don't mind. I want to share with her what we are. And share our heritage with…there are others I'd like to tell as well. Trustworthy beings that you'll meet soon."

"Well of course you will. But you didn't bring her this time?" He shook his head. "It's no matter, no matter at all. You will next time. Bring her I mean. Is she lovely? Breedable?"

"Kimdar, what is wrong with you? Of course she's lovely, and what a thing to ask. She'll have us plenty of babies to hold." His mom looked at him. "You will have plenty of babies for us, won't you, son?"

"If she agrees." His mother smiled at him. "Her family is large; she has five sisters, and some of them have mates. One recently had a child."

"Bring them all." His father bellowed for his first man. "Get the rooms aright. We're having company. And food. Lots of food for…are they all wolves?"

"Yes." He looked at his mom when his dad went to see to the food. He took her hand into his and kissed it. "Mom, I need an opal. It's her name, and I need an opal that will pale in comparison to her, but be beautiful for her."

"I'll take care of it for you. It will be awaiting you when you return to your home." He nodded and stood up. "You leave us so soon? When will you return? Soon? If not, your father may just come for you both if you don't come back with her as soon as possible."

"Give me a week. I'll need to prepare her and them for this." She looked at him with a cocked brow. "I've never told any of them what we…they have met Ursula, but she, too, is a mystery to them."

"I will talk to her then. See what she can tell me of your new family." He moved toward the door after giving his mother a hug and a kiss. She stopped him as he was exiting their room. "Sloan, do you think she'll like us?"

"Mom, she will love you."

# Chapter 13

"I don't understand." Sloan only smiled at her, but she wanted to bash him over the head. "You're telling me that not only are your parents still around, but they want to meet me? Why?"

"Why? Because I love you." Not a reason and she told him that. "They want to meet my mate. They want to be able to tell you all sorts of things I did as a child, embarrass me, and make me feel as if I may never return."

"I don't need stories of you as a child. Just take a picture of me and...where are they living, anyway?" He mumbled something and she took a step toward him. "Please tell me you didn't just say in another realm."

"It's where I was created." Opal had to sit down. This was just too much. Not only had he just told her that his parents wanted to meet her and her family, but they also wanted them to stay for a time. But in another realm? Not fucking likely.

"I don't want to go." She didn't really like the way she sounded like a five-year-old, but she wasn't going. "Tell them to come here and see me. That way if they don't like me, they can go back home and I won't be stuck with my family there loving the place and never being invited back."

"You're going to love them. I told them all about you."
That made her groan. "I've already made arrangements
with your family. They're packing as we speak."

"Oh, you didn't." He said that he had indeed. "Do
they—your parents—know that we're all wolves? That
we...that we require daylight and meat?" She was grasping
at straws and they both knew it.

"They are making arrangements now for you all." She
sat down, then stood again. "We leave in the morning."

She turned slowly to look at him. In the morning.
Glancing at the clock, she saw that it was just after seven in
the evening. She was supposed to be ready to go in the
morning.

"Were you going to tell me at all?" He shrugged and
laid down on the bed. She liked him there most of the time,
but for now, she wanted to murder him. "I'm not going to
have time for you if I have to pack."

"Come here, Opal. I need to taste you." Her body
always responded to him when he spoke to her in that low,
sexy voice of his. "Strip down for me. Take off everything
and let me watch you play."

"Play?" He pulled her vibrator from under his pillow
and turned it on. "I'm not in the mood."

"You are. Very much so." He sat up and told her to
come to him. He only ran the tip of the vibrating thing over
her belly, but she moaned. "See? I knew that you needed
this. Let me watch you while you bring yourself to peak."

"I don't want to." But she was pulling her blouse over
her head even as he sat on the edge of the bed to watch her.
He touched her bare skin everywhere she exposed. And by
the time she was down to just her panties, she was close to
coming with or without the thing in his hand, and she
didn't care who knew it.

He handed her the purple dildo and leaned back. She could see how hard he was, and it made her want to make him come just like he was. When she ran the tip over her hard nipple, Opal moaned loudly and then slid it down to her pussy. She knew he was watching her, and when he sat up and pulled his cock free of his pants, she watched him slide his hand up and down while she pressed the cock onto her clit.

The climax was hard; it took her breath away with the speed in which she came. When he dropped to his knees in front of her, she started to hand it to him but he told her no.

"I'm going to drink the juices that run from you. Lick that pretty clit while you play with it. It's so hard now that it is begging for me to nibble on it." She moaned again as he spread her nether lips open. Touching the cock to her clit again had her screaming out his name as she came again. When Sloan suckled her, she cried out again when she released.

"Fuck me." He turned her to the bed and laid her over it. She spread her legs wide for him as she slid the cock into her. He never stopped sucking on her, and when she came again, he stood up and tore his clothes off. He stood over her gloriously naked and hard.

Sitting up, she took him into her mouth while the vibrator slid in and out of her pussy. She was being fucked at both ends and she was close to coming again. His hand curling into her hair had her moaning, and when he began to fuck her mouth, she fucked herself harder.

"Come for me." She moaned when he told her again to come. She didn't want to come this way...she wanted him deep inside of her. When he tore her head from his cock, she moaned and he fisted his cock. "Come for me, baby. I want you to come."

"Fuck me. Please, I beg you. I want to feel your cock buried inside of me." He turned her over so fast that she lost her toy, but as soon as he had her leaned over the bed, her ass in the air, she felt it roll over her again. As his cock moved to her pussy, she nearly begged him to let her come when he pulled back. She waited while he stood behind her.

"I can't decide if I want to fuck you this way or turn you over and eat you until you come." She moaned when the cock he was still moving over her touched her clit. "Fuck it, I need to come inside of you."

He entered her hard. She braced her hands on the bed and felt him pull out then slam back into her harder than before. Every time he did this, every time he entered her harder, she felt her wolf scream at her to let her out. When Opal came, screaming out his name as he sank his fangs into her, Opal reached between her legs and cupped his balls. He roared out his release and held her down while he marked her again. Opal fell forward with his weight when he came the second time.

The only time she opened her eyes after that was when she felt him lift her into his arms and then settle her onto their bed. The new bed had arrived today and she'd forgotten to ask him how he liked it. Just as she was drifting back to sleep, he kissed her.

"I love you. Will you marry me?" She whispered yes, knowing that he was joking, and closed her eyes. Tomorrow she'd laugh about it. But for now? She was exhausted.

~~~

Sloan held his breath when she walked into the castle. Last night he'd taken a chance that she'd say yes, but now...well, now he wasn't so sure. He'd more or less tricked her. And now that it was time to tell her the truth, he was as nervous as he'd ever been. His dad came forward, and he realized something he'd forgotten in all the bustle of getting here.

"My father the king." She turned to him slowly. "I forgot to tell you. My mom is the queen, too."

"Really?" She turned to his dad and was engulfed in his arms like she weighed no more than a feather. Then he kissed her on the mouth and set her back down. His dad looked at him.

"She's lovely, just lovely. Just like I knew she'd be." He slapped him on the back as he moved them toward the receiving hall. "I'm glad you decided to have the wedding here. Makes it so much nicer to have everyone here when we have so much…what's wrong?"

"Dad?" He knew the exact moment his dad realized what had happened. "I meant to tell her last night. After I proposed, but I got sidetracked."

"I just bet you did." Sloan was a grown man, older than most anyone he knew, certainly old enough not to blush when his father guessed why he'd been distracted. "Lovely way to spend the night. And day, too, if you want to know the truth. Keep that up and there'll be grandchildren before the wedding."

"There will be no wedding." Opal turned to glare at him. "How could you? How could you do this to me? And my family? I suppose they know too."

"Yes." He felt stupid and then he got mad. "I was trying to make you happy, damn it."

"Sloan." His mom had a way about her that made him want to crawl into a hole, never to come out. He knew the tone of her voice too. Like Opal, he'd disappointed her.

"Her family is on their way here. I messed up." His mom gathered Opal into her arms and started away with her. Sloan looked at his dad. "I really fucked this up."

"Maybe." That wasn't at all helpful. "Then again, maybe not. Your mother will fix this. See if she doesn't. In the meantime, let's you and I have a walk about. I need to ask you a few things, and there are a few people here that want to see you. We've invited Ursula and that man of yours...what's his name?"

"Rufus?" *Christ*, he thought, *could this day get any worse?* More than likely he'd bet it could. When they entered his father's office, Sloan took the seat across from him. Within minutes they were joined by two other men, neither of whom he knew. Then after that, Allen, Blair, Thad, and Quentin joined them. For some reason, Sloan had a feeling he was being set up.

"I'd like to ask you all to raise a glass to my son." Each man took a glass, but only the one his father held and the two men were filled with a red liquid, while the rest were filled with champagne. "To him and his lovely bride. May they have centuries of a wonderful life together. And many a grandchild for me to spoil."

Everyone drank, and then in a tradition of his kind, each glass was tossed into a large open container made of crystal that sat on his desk. He watched as the glass former stepped into the yard with the container and began to heat the glass.

"What's he doing?" Sloan looked over at Allen when he asked. "I know what he's doing really, just not what he's doing."

Sloan laughed. "Each glass within the framework has a small part of us on it, sort of a part of the whole. Our DNA, our prints from our fingers. Anything that makes us what we are is now going to be melted together and formed. I'm not sure what it will be; only the blower and the glass knows."

They each watched as the man took the glass, now molten hot, and started to mix it around. Colors were added, dark blues and reds of his crest and a deep green to be added for the color of the Erickson clan. They all watched as the glass was added to a long pipe and the process began. Large bamboo sticks were used to mold it, smaller stones on the tips of more glass were pressed against the form to make textures and lines. No one said a word as the man worked for nearly forty minutes on making the thing come to shape.

"Well, I'll be damned." Sloan smiled, thinking that Thad had it right. The form had taken on a shape that he'd been surprised about as well. Then when the former set the piece aside, he pulled out a second piece of stone and put it on the back of the wolves. The opal melted down over the back of the smaller of the two of them and settled over it like a coat. Sloan looked at his dad.

"Did he know?" His dad shook his head. "You had to have told him that Opal and I are wolves?"

"No. I gave him the opal and asked if he'd try to work it in, but I never told him anything. You know we wouldn't be able to shape your future like that." Blair asked him what he meant. "The glass, as fragile as a heart, can be shaped in any way you make it. But if you let it go freely, form around the other heart that it knows, things—great things—will come of it. And once it is together, cooled into something hard, then that love will last for longer than lives can be lived."

"I like that." Quentin smiled as he looked over at him. "That's very nice. A great way to start your marriage. She'll love it."

"If'n she don't bash it over his stupid head." They all looked at Rufus, who stood in the doorway. "You might want to come on out here, boss. That mate of yours has got herself all tangled up in a mess."

He moved as quickly as he could and stopped when he saw her. She was standing in the middle of the receiving room with a sword in one hand and his mother shoved behind her with the other. Sloan had no idea what was going on, but the further he walked into the room, the more he was scared.

"Opal?" She turned to look at him. "What's going on? Why are you trying to...why are you trying to do whatever it is you're doing?"

"They were going to kill her." He looked at his mom, then back at the people standing bunched near a wall. "You should have seen that first one. They were going to cut her up."

"I was only doing my job, Master Sloan." He nodded to the man that spoke. "We tried our best to make her understand, but she...she's not hearing us."

It took him several seconds, precious seconds really, to realize that they were speaking the language of his people. He asked the young man if he spoke English. His head shook hard and he looked slightly insulted.

"She doesn't understand us or what you're trying to tell her." He moved slowly to Opal as he continued talking to the man. "She's protecting my mom because she fears you're going to harm her. Instead of being upset with her, you should be thankful that she was so brave against so many."

He pulled her into his arms when he reached her. She sobbed gently against his chest as he looked at his mom. The smile on her face was wide. He had no clue why she'd think any of this was funny.

"She was going to kill them all and not think a thing about it." He nodded, noting that his mom was speaking in English now. "She had not a single clue what was going on, yet she came in here when they were readying me for her and immediately took offense."

"They were hurting you." Opal turned in his arms to look at his mom. "You were hurt and bleeding. What the hell was I supposed to think?"

"Just what you did. That I'd been hurt. I had been hurt, but due to my own stupidity, not what they did. I was with the ravens. You know how they can be, don't you?" She shook her head. "Well, they can be a might on the bitchy side when I've not been out to play with them in a while. And with your wedding coming up, I sort of—"

"There is no wedding." The room, everyone there, dropped to the floor when Opal cut off his mom. "I didn't say I'd marry him. And I don't even know if I like him very much right now."

His mom laughed, a big booming laugh that had the servants looking up then back down again. She pulled Opal into her arms and hugged her tightly as they made their way to the other end of the room. Sloan was still standing there when Blair patted him on the back.

"Sucks, huh?" He looked at Blair. "Not being in control. My dad does that to me all the time. I think I have a handle on the situation, and he comes into the room and it all goes to shit. But in a good way."

"She just went with her and left me standing here." Blair nodded and they both moved back to the room where the rest of them were. "How does one survive this? I mean, is there a manual or a reference book I can use?"

"Nope." Allen handed him a glass of beer. He eyed the glass carefully before taking it. "I heard tell you are able to eat all sorts of things now."

"Not cheese. It doesn't agree with me." He looked over at his dad, who was talking with his brothers-in-law. "My dad will make friends with anyone."

"He would, I bet. And he'd kill them if they fucked with what was his." That was true as well, and he told Allen so. "You're a good deal like him, I think. Not just in looks, though there you're almost twins. But you both have that same slow manner that makes one think you might be a little on the slow side."

"Thanks." Allen laughed and Sloan looked around the room again. "She said no. I asked her last night and she said yes, but today…today she's saying no to me."

"You asked her? She said yes?" Sloan said yes. "Then I'll talk to her." Behind Allen, his son was shaking his head, cutting his fingers across his throat, and mouthing the word "no." But instead of heeding his friend's advice, he nodded. What harm could come of it, right?

The rest of the afternoon was spent on him roaming the castle for Opal. She was upset with him, he knew that. For what, he wasn't really sure, but she was blocking him. He heard several times what a lovely person she was, but he could not find her. He just wanted to go home and start the day over.

But for reasons he could not fathom, he was pretty sure he wasn't going to be able to do that for a while yet.

# Chapter 14

The dress was...Opal knew that the word amazing was inadequate, but that's just what it was. And the longer she looked at it, the more she wanted to try it on. But she only stared at it as Calane, Sloan's mom, talked about things that she'd done that week. Most of it, nearly all of it, centered on her getting the place ready for them.

"Do you want to try it on?" She looked at Calane, who smiled as she continued. "It's for you. I know you kind of figured that out, but I didn't want to push. But I'd love to see you in it more than I can tell you."

"My grandmother would love this. It looks so much like the one she had picked out for my own mom when her and my dad got married. But they ended up getting married by a justice of the peace. He didn't want to wait." Opal fingered the lace that made up nearly ninety percent of the dress. "How did you know my size?"

"I didn't. That's my dress." Opal turned to look at the tiny woman who was now seated at a large desk. "It's magical, like the rest of this place. Whoever it chooses...and I know that's hard to understand...but whoever the dress chooses to wear it, it will accommodate the size for them. Ursula made it for me. And when I asked her if you may wear it, she told me only if the dress said it was okay. Very strange, but if you spend much time here, you'll get used to it."

"The faerie." Calane shook her head. "There's another named for her? I have to tell you, I just love her name. But I thought that someone said she was faerie."

"No. I mean Ursula isn't a faerie, and I love her name as well. Her sister, Ysane, is faerie. Most think Ursula is, but she is Jinn. Do you know what that is?" Opal felt her hair dance on her arm. "She's not evil, child, she's just her. And over the centuries, she's become quite good at being what she is."

"She's said to be...to be a monster. Her kind kills without mercy and does it in ways that the person will suffer the most." Calane nodded and smiled. "Then I'm confused. How could someone make something this lovely and be Jinn?"

"I'm sure if people were to know that you're a wolf, they'd wonder the same of you." That was true. Even her own kind were considered savages. She looked at the dress with more respect. "I would very much like to see you try it on. And your sisters are here as well. They are being put into their rooms as we speak. Would you like them to meet you here?"

"Yes." Opal felt tears fill her eyes. "I know it's silly, but...this is really too much. I'm terrified if you want to know the truth. And being wife to Sloan, it's not necessary. I can be his mate and that'll be fine. He will tire of me soon, and then what will I have? Memories that will haunt me? Dreams of a man that I loved with all of my heart? I don't think I'd survive that."

"You will because he loves you a great deal." Opal nodded. "You love him too. That is more than most people ever get in their life. He's a wonderful man if I do say so myself. And hurting because he's hurt you."

"He is a wonderful man. And very stubborn. I wonder where he might have gotten that from." Calane immediately said his father, and Opal laughed. "I would guess he got a great deal from both of you."

"Mayhap. But that's not the issue, is it? What are you afraid of?" So many things she wanted to say, but Calane smiled as she answered her own question. "Commitment? You mentioned that he'd tire of you. Do you think to tire of him as well?"

"No. Never. I know in my head that can't happen, but my heart tells me that he'll get bored with me. I'm not really the...I'm more of a finish work and go home to a nice little house in the woods kind of girl."

"I'm reasonably sure that you don't have a small house, and while it might be near woods, there is more than you expected of it. So, from this I'm to gather it's his money." Opal sat on the bed and nodded. "He does have a great deal of it. More than you can spend in all your lifetimes if he never made another penny. Then there are the things and money that he has here. I'm not sure what the equivalent is to people of your realm, but I would say that it's a great deal more than he has there."

"You're not helping." Calane laughed again. "I don't know how to be rich and glamourous."

"Glamour you don't need to work at. Rich? Why do you have to know how to be rich? Do you enjoy having nice things? Sloan tells me you have a lovely shop. Do you like being able to sell pretty things? Have things in it that no one else has?" She nodded. "Then you are well on your way to learning how to be rich."

Opal sat there staring around the room. She had no idea, but she thought this was Sloan's room. Getting up, she wandered around, picking up the things that were his and putting them back. When she came across a small flower in a picture frame, she turned to Calane.

"He grew that. Long, long ago, but I remember it like it was yesterday. He'd been out with the gardener. Several times a day he'd leave here and go out and hunt the poor man down. And he'd spend hours with him. It's a small wonder that the man continued to work for us. But Sloan had begged him to plant a garden. He didn't like vegetables, but he knew that I loved flowers. After weeks and weeks of him out working his little plot of land, he came in to tell us that he had a plant growing. It wasn't the only one he had, but it was this one that was doing the best. One that he'd been able to create with his own hands." She got up and came to her and touched the flower that was hidden behind the glass. "A month later he came in with this in his hand. He handed it to me with such a flourish you would have thought it was a bag of gems. And to me, it was worth more than that. He'd grown this just for me. Do you know what this is?"

"No. It's the most beautiful flower I've ever seen. The colors are almost...they looked like a moonstone." Calane nodded. "Can we grow them on earth? I have a sister that owns a plant shop. She'd make a fortune selling these, as I'm sure no one else in her line of work has them."

"I have no idea. And it's called Opal's Dream." Opal looked at her. "I was surprised myself when he told us your name. All these years, all these lifetimes, and here you are, his own Opal's Dream."

Her sisters and grandmother came in then. The baby was passed to Calane, who immediately said she was going to adopt him as her own grandchild. Sapphire talked Opal into trying on the dress, and before she knew it, she was dressed as a bride. Looking in the mirrors that had been set up for her, she looked at the woman staring back at her.

"You've never looked more beautiful." She looked at her grandmother. "Are you going to marry him?"

"Yes." Her grandmother kissed her cheek. She looked up when Sapphire said her name. The flowers that were handed to her nearly made her weep. "They're mine."

As her sisters began to dress, Opal moved out into the garden off from the room. She was staring up at one of the trees in full bloom when she heard someone say her name. Ursula came to stand before her.

"You are very lovely, my lady." Opal nodded and sat down when she did. "I have a wedding gift for you. You must understand that by accepting this gift, you will have a part of me."

"What is it?" She didn't answer, but then Opal didn't really think she would. "Does Sloan have the same gift from you?"

"He does, my lady." She told her she was just plain Opal. "Nah, you are more than plain anyone. You will be queen here some day and in turn, your husband, my friend, the king. You are both destined to be worshiped by those you lead and cherished by all who know you. I should like to tell you something, if you do not mind."

"I'm not ready for that." Ursula laughed. "Please tell me and then I'll let you know if I can accept the gift. If you do me one favor first."

"First, my tale." Opal nodded. "Long ago there were six gems. Not unlike your sisters and you, but these were stones, not ones of flesh as the six of you are. As they made their way together, each of them coming from different parts of the realm in which we live, they memorized their adventures, their trials, and their tribulations. Each, you see, had a different life than the one that they knew they were destined to have. A life that would be safe, wonderfully magical and full of love. The opal, one like you, was the bravest of them all. Her story has been passed down to each Jinn, until I was asked to give it to you."

The stone she put into Opal's palm when she took her hand was warm. Opal felt the tremendous weight of it and held it up to the sun to see its clarity and perfection. But in the middle, shining back at her, were twinkling lights. She looked at Ursula, who smiled.

"She took the stones into herself to protect them. Some of them were stronger than her, others smarter, but none of them were as brave as the opal. It is why, when all of them came together, that she was chosen above the other five to keep them safe." Ursula took the stone again and tapped it gently against the hard seat. It split in two and spilled out not just the other gems—each of which one of her sisters was named for—but twelve of the most beautiful opals she'd ever seen. "Your daughters will each have one. You'll have no sons, but twelve daughters to carry on the task set before you this day. And my gift to you, should you take it, will help you in ways that you will need to protect the gems of your flesh."

The gems were poured into her hand, and Opal felt the connection to them immediately. She looked at the Jinn and knew for as long as she lived, this woman would mean everything to her. She nodded and asked if she could ask her favor now.

"Anything, my lady. You need only to wish it, and it will by yours." Opal wasn't sure about all that, but she took her hand and felt the power wash over her. It was a gentle rain feeling, soft and warm and full of hope and promise. "And your favor?"

"You're going to be one of my bridesmaids." The look of horror on Ursula's face was priceless. Opal was still laughing when a dress was brought for her to put on. As soon as they were all assembled, Sloan was informed that the wedding was about to take place. Opal just hoped that he didn't back out now.

~~~

He'd never been more terrified and relaxed in his life. His bride, his Opal, was going to be his wife in a matter of minutes. Sloan stood with the men who had come to mean so much to him, and wondered if they'd all felt this way about the women they had married. His friend Thad came forward just as he was ready to go and find Opal, just to be sure she was still going through with this.

"She is." He nodded and felt his body relax just a little more. "I heard from Jade. She said to tell you that if you fuck this up, she's going to cut your balls off and serve them to you for the rest of your life. I'm not sure how she'll manage that, but I believe her."

"Me too." He let out a long breath. "She is going to be my wife. After all this time, I have not just a mate, but one that I love very much."

"Who would have thought it?" Thad laughed. "You're a lucky man. We all are. Even Rufus is pretty lucky, even though I doubt very much he'll find him a wife."

"He'd run so quickly that she'd never catch him." He watched Rufus pull at his tie again. The fact that he was willing to stand in with him made him love the guy all that much more. "I'd very much like it if you were to be my best man."

Thad looked shocked for several seconds, then nodded. "It would be an honor. Did you know that Opal asked Angie to be her maid of honor? She is beside herself with excitement. But I wanted to tell you something...I know that...hell buddy, we've been friends for a long time. I think having you as a brother-in-law will be fantastic."

He handed him the ring he'd approved from his mother. She'd sent him five rings, but this one he loved. Sloan decided that the other rings would be saved for when their children were born. Thad whistled loudly as he held the ring that would bond them as husband and wife.

"My mother designed it. She said she loved it for its simplicity as well as its beauty. I think it suits Opal more than anything I could have purchased for her." Thad nodded.

The ring was carved from an opal of such a beautiful shade of creamy blue that he wondered if his mother had made it. It was a darker opal with many streaks of white and blues running throughout it. But it was the heart that caught one's attention; it had seemingly been made in the stone just to be used for this purpose. Thad put it into his pocket.

As soon as they were assembled in the large room, Sloan looked out over the crowd. He'd never seen so many people before. As he watched, more and more seemed to spill out everywhere, including the gardens where he and the men now stood. As soon as the harpist started playing, he looked to the back of the room.

Unlike Earth's traditional weddings, the bride came out with the maids. Each of them, and in this case her sisters and Ursula, came out carrying a small part of her train. Angie, holding a basket of leaves that meant long life to his kind, kept looking back at her aunts to make sure they were in line. Opal's grandmother was giving her to him and held her hand. It was the bouquet of flowers that made his breath catch. They were his Opal's Dream.

When Opal was standing beside him, he reached for her and kissed her. Much to the amusement of the room, he was told to wait his turn. When Opal blushed at him, he kissed her again just to keep it there. The room was called to order and they all looked at his mom and dad.

"Today I am honored to give my son a wife. And in the tradition of our kind, I've been asked to preside over their union. Today...today I gain something very precious to us. We have a daughter to call our own. And a large family to go along with her. It's more than any man could hope or ever wish for." His dad wiped at a tear and smiled at him. "Sloan, son of Kimdar and Calane, Rulers of Darkness Realm, do you wish to spend your eternity and beyond with Opal Grace Erickson, daughter of earth, sister to many and loved by everyone?"

"Yes." His dad nodded at him and he looked at Opal. "I love you with all my heart. I really didn't think I could, what with you being so stubborn and all, but you made me realize how lonely I've been, how sad I'd be if you were gone, and how much I could love someone coming into my life."

"Good boy." His dad looked at Opal. "Opal, my dear, would you care for my son, love him throughout all eternity, give him the greatest gift of all kind, and keep him as close to your heart as you can?"

"I can't." The room seemed to still and his heart did the same. "I can't keep him close to my heart, because he has it all. I love him with all that I am and will for the rest of my life. I want children with him, lives with him, and I want to share all that we can be with him."

His dad leaned over and kissed her cheek and then hugged her. Sloan could only stare as his dad sobbed on his new daughter-in-law's shoulder for several minutes as he thanked her for being her. When he stood again, Sloan looked out over the room again and noticed there was not a dry eye in the place, and that even Rufus was wiping at his cheeks.

"As I was saying." His dad looked at him. "You've got yourself a winner here, son. You know that, right?"

"I do." His dad told him to give her the ring. He looked at Opal once again as he slipped it over her finger and then kissed it. "I love you with all of my being. I will love you forever."

He pulled her to him and leaned down to her mouth. He wanted it to be romantic, he wanted her to be breathless afterwards, but all he could think about was claiming his bride. So without any thought to the people in the room, he kissed her, then lifted her body to his and left the room with her nearly wrapped around him.

The suite that they had been given was big, not that he cared. There was a bed, and right now, that was all he could think about. Lifting his head just enough to look at her, he smiled. She smiled right back.

"I couldn't wait." She nodded and he kissed her again. "I need you. I need to be deep inside of you more than I need my next breath."

"Hurry." Sloan stripped her down. He wasn't gentle about it either. When she was standing in front of him with just her thigh high stockings and her heels on, he had to step back or attack.

"Christ." Opal grinned at him and he moved to her. But she laid back on the bed before he could touch her. Sloan pulled off his jacket and tossed it to the floor, then his tie and shirt. He was standing in just his pants when she reached for him.

Sloan loved this woman. He tried his best to show her how much, but she tore his pants open, breaking the zipper and the button off before he could do much more than watch. As soon as his cock was freed, she was taking him deep into her mouth. Sloan's eyes rolled to the back of his head.

Her mouth did things to him that had him moaning and begging her for release. When she finally lifted her head from his cock with a tiny pop, he stared down at her. He was lightheaded, dizzy even. All his blood was centered in one place, and he was in deep need of release.

"I need to make love to you." Opal laid back and spread her legs for him. She was so wet that her thighs were damp, as was the bed beneath her. Dropping to his knees, he put her thighs up over his shoulders and spread her wider with his fingers. Leaning in, he suckled her clit into his mouth and bit her. Her release flooded his mouth with her cream.

Lapping greedily, he drank from her. She came several more times before he knew that if he didn't stop now, he never would. Moving up her body, biting her and then licking the wound closed, he took her breast deep into his mouth and sank his fangs into her. When she cried out again, Sloan filled her with his cock and lifted her ass to him to take her deeper and harder.

"Come for me." She dug her nails into his back and screamed again. When she licked his throat, her fangs scraping over his pounding pulse, he moved in and out of her faster, pounding her hard, knowing that when she bit him, sank those lovely fangs into him, he was going to come harder than he ever had before. But he was wrong.

She bit him and his world splintered, his mind shattered, and his entire being, his body and all, came to an earth-shattering halt before he came back together with a sonic boom. He sank his fangs into her, biting her wherever he could until her blood filled his mouth, his body, and Christ, even his heart. Sloan felt his world pinpoint into a single white dot before he was brought under.

He was out for only seconds. When he looked down at his wife, the love of his life, he could see that she, too, had succumbed to the darkness, and held her to him as he laid there. She stirred beneath him and he looked down again, and noticed the color of her eyes immediately.

"Did Ursula touch you?" She nodded. "She gave you a gift. Did she tell you what it was? Did she explain what she'd done?"

"No. She said you had the same gift and I...what did she do?" Sloan was almost afraid to tell her. Excitement ran over his body, but fear too that she'd be upset. "Sloan?"

"We're going to have a child." Opal nodded, but he was sure she didn't understand. "I mean, we just created a child. And because of the glow in your eyes, the color of them, I'd say that this child will have things you and I don't. Magic, and a great deal of it."

"She told me. The story of the opal, she told me." He shifted when she did and she lay over him now. "I'm guessing I should learn to ask her from now on, huh?"

"I'd say that's a good thing for both of us." He lifted her chin up and looked at her. "Your eyes are blue now. Like a Jinn. I wonder how much you have from this."

"Does it matter?"

He shook his head, and she laid her head back on his chest. Sloan tried to think if he was upset or not, but all he could think of was that Opal was going to have his baby.

"Sloan, do you think we should go back to the wedding? Your parents have been planning this, so we should at least make an appearance."

"We should." But neither of them moved. "I love you, Opal Crane. I will love you forever."

"And I love you." This time when she sat up she moved off him and stood before him. "But I'm starved. I need to find something to fill me up if we're going to make love on our wedding night."

He was still laughing when he walked into the reception room. They were greeted with a loud cheer, and he kissed her soundly when someone shouted for him to do so. Sloan doubted that he'd ever been this happy, and wondered if he'd stay this way for the rest of his life. He looked at Opal. Yes, he decided. He would.

# About the Author

Kathi Barton, author of the bestselling series Force of Nature, lives in Nashport, Ohio with her husband Paul. In addition to writing full time Kathi likes to spend time with her eight grandkids, three children and three children-in-laws. She writes to relax and have fun.

Her muse, a cross between Jimmy Stewart and Hugh Jackman brings them to life for her readers in a way that has them coming back time and again for more. Her favorite genre is paranormal romance with a great deal of spice. You can visit Kathi on line and drop her an email if you'd like. She loves hearing from her fans. aaronskiss@gmail.com.

Follow Kathi on her blog: http://kathisbartonauthor.blogspot.com/